A hellbomb was loaded and ready to fly

Bolan gave the lay of the land a last look. All told, it was as good a place as any to start a small war.

The Executioner slid down the low rise on his belly, taking the M-16 with him. Out of sight, he chose the closest team of three and went off hunting.

It was time to hurl a few more bodies onto the conveyor belt of death. With enough skill, determination and a little bit of luck, Bolan hoped that when the dust settled he wasn't stretched out for the buzzards.

The enemy had initially called the game, done its damnedest so far to cash him out for the final ride. Viewed in that light, Bolan was gong to give it back to them in spades, nothing but blood and thunder on the horizon.

It was blitz time.

MACK BOLAN ®
The Executioner

DON PENDLETON'S
THE EXECUTIONER®
FIRE WIND

A GOLD EAGLE BOOK FROM
WORLDWIDE®

TORONTO • NEW YORK • LONDON
AMSTERDAM • PARIS • SYDNEY • HAMBURG
STOCKHOLM • ATHENS • TOKYO • MILAN
MADRID • WARSAW • BUDAPEST • AUCKLAND

First edition February 2002
ISBN 0-373-64279-2

Special thanks and acknowledgment to
Dan Schmidt for his contribution to this work.

FIRE WIND

Printed In U.S.A.

The life of humanity upon this planet may come to an end, and a very terrible end. But I would have you notice that this end is threatened in our time not by anything that the universe may do to us, but only by what man may do to himself.

—John Haynes Holmes,
1879–1964

A warrior has a job to do. It is his duty to slay the enemy, and sometimes it's done in the most brutal way possible. Yet at the same time, the warrior can still maintain his humanity where noncombatants are concerned. It's what separates us from the butchers.

—Mack Bolan

THE
MACK BOLAN®
LEGEND

Nothing less than a war could have fashioned the destiny of the man called Mack Bolan. Bolan earned the Executioner title in the jungle hell of Vietnam.

But this soldier also wore another name—Sergeant Mercy. He was so tagged because of the compassion he showed to wounded comrades-in-arms and Vietnamese civilians.

Mack Bolan's second tour of duty ended prematurely when he was given emergency leave to return home and bury his family, victims of the Mob. Then he declared a one-man war against the Mafia.

He confronted the Families head-on from coast to coast, and soon a hope of victory began to appear. But Bolan had broken society's every rule. That same society started gunning for this elusive warrior—to no avail.

So Bolan was offered amnesty to work within the system against terrorism. This time, as an employee of Uncle Sam, Bolan became Colonel John Phoenix. With a command center at Stony Man Farm in Virginia, he and his new allies—Able Team and Phoenix Force—waged relentless war on a new adversary: the KGB.

But when his one true love, April Rose, died at the hands of the Soviet terror machine, Bolan severed all ties with Establishment authority.

Now, after a lengthy lone-wolf struggle and much soul-searching, the Executioner has agreed to enter an "arm's-length" alliance with his government once more, reserving the right to pursue personal missions in his Everlasting War.

Prologue

It would prove a bad way to die, if what Burt Jenkins glimpsed ahead was any indication of the end. After long and hellish stints in two foreign prisons, death by any means—quick and violent, or protracted misery on the way to the grave—wasn't a calling the former Army Ranger wanted to hold near and dear to the heart. Which was why Jenkins suffered through lumbering around in the dark, cocooned like some trapped bug in the cumbersome bulk of the hazardous material biosuit.

The geek team, as he had come to think of the so-called specialists, those slight men with their curious childlike stares, bland faces and, in his opinion, myopic scope of the real world where blood and guts were his bottom line, was advancing on the shadowy lumps stacked at the end of the gorge.

Jenkins felt somewhat silly the next moment, toting around the HK MP-5 subgun in gloved hands. If a problem did crop up, he might as well get caught with his shorts down around his ankles, tripping about while attempting to strike back at some wandering snoop, seeing himself clanking after an intruder in robotic slow motion. The Geekmaster, he recalled, feeling a cold trickle of sweat arcing down his forehead, maybe told him the char-coal-based material of this state-of-the-art biosuit was much lighter and more mobile than the old rubberized version, but he still saw himself as a mummy with a gun.

Or a potential clumsy target.

Jenkins watched as the four-man geek team checked the illuminated dials of their digitalized dosimeters. The com link inside his helmet bubble crackled to life, the head specialist, Timson, sounding damn near giddy with the progress report. The wristwatch Geiger coun-ters crackled over the frequency like a mad swarm of chittering insects, further stoking Jenkins's agitation and paranoia.

Before they launched themselves into a round of self-congratulation while once more snapping on the flashlights to inspect the fruits of the experiment's grim reward, Jenkins took a moment to get his bearings, look around, search the dark. Angola, Sudan and Pakistan had long since taught him to never trust the silent night. Here, knowing what he knew much less seeing what he saw put his teeth on edge to the point where he thought he might nearly start imagining the rocks themselves could come alive with armed shadows. What could he do? he wondered. Nothing, he knew, except go with the program, since he'd been saved way back when, re-cruited, in fact, paid fat cash in advance and promised his own pot of gold at the end of this dirty rainbow.

Three days around the clock now they had marked off this little slice of southwestern Colorado, straddling the county lines of Dolores and Montezuma. Before venturing out of their prefab but lead-lined, hermeti-cally sealed command center at the opposite end of the gorge, past the barrier wall of piñons and juniper, Jenkins had given the order for the two black choppers to do a thorough sweep of the area. The posted signs at selected points around their open four-square-mile box of staked claim may or may not hold back prying eyes, but he wasn't about to trust a few choice and threatening words to do the job. No Trespassing. Property of United States Government. Use of Deadly Force Authorized. Well, all that standard dire noise aside, he'd heard the tales himself, and not even Federal Regulation Number 795 discouraged the curious from wandering too close to Area 51, where they were supposedly black-engineering UFOs and deep-freezing little gray men.

The rotor wash was something of a muffled buzz inside his helmet, but he spotted his choppers, rearing like carnivorous birds over the gorge, spewing up a dust storm. They were armed with twin GAU-2B-A 7.62 mm miniguns in the turret, he knew, deciding they looked like flying dragons in their hybrid cross between the old Huey and a Black Hawk. The blackbirds, winged with pylons that housed seventy-six 2.75-inch rockets, crisscrossed from north to south, search beams dancing over the maze of gulleys, mesas, sandstone cliffs around and beyond the gorge. What little he knew about this lunar landscape spooked him even more. The Anasazi Indians were believed the first human beings to set foot here, digging out pueblo cities in the cliff sides some fifteen centuries ago, if he recalled right. For reasons no one knew, the Anasazi, which, he'd read somewhere, was Navaho for "Enemies of Our Ancestors," had seemed to vanish almost without a trace seven hundred years or so back. Enemies of whom or what? he wondered. Whose ancestors? Against his will he pictured some of the drawings he'd seen while on recon for trespassers. Before vanishing altogether the Anasazi had either etched or painted vague shapes on the rock of small figures with large black eyes and bubble heads shaped sort of like grasshoppers. What the hell was he thinking, and almost laughed out loud at the idiotic flight of fancy, then he found himself in present time, and his gaze fell on the dead cattle.

And almost wished he was still back in the dungeons of Angola or Pakistan, rotting out the years and cheating death at every corner before he was mysteriously bailed out by an even more mysterious benefactor with cash to burn and armed with a plan for the future of Burt Jenkins the mercenary.

"Incredible," he heard Timson state, the specialist holding up an arm to indicate they should stop and view the sights in the same awe that froze his nondescript cherub face inside the bubble. "I'm reading rads, gentlemen, at...six-ten and climbing deeper into the hot zone. One hundred percent fatalities. Less than two full days' exposure."

It was true. None of the twelve cattle shipped in by the black semi with government plates even twitched. Total annihilation—or success, depending on the viewpoint—stared the ex-Ranger back from the fenced-in corrugated pen. Jenkins saw gummy drool pooling beneath gaping jaws, black eyes bugged out from fever that had burned up their insides thanks to an invisible man-made fire.

The winds of hell on earth, Jenkins thought, as Timson prattled on about the prevailing gust from the east, a steady twenty-something mile-per-hour sheet that had blown across the western slope and plateau country from the towering wall of the Rocky Mountains the past day, as if Mother Nature had provided aid to their ghoul's task here.

Jenkins really wanted nothing more than for one of them to shut the device down, then shower up and scrub at the mobile decon unit since they were all standing in a hot zone he feared might have made Chernobyl a mere marshmallow roast. Instead they babbled about ionizing radiation, roentgens and rad levels driven by the wind, dispersal radius, NIA—or neutron-induced activity, one of them spelling that out as if for his benefit. This was a freak show, he thought. And these were employees of Uncle Sam? He checked that judgment right away, since he was also under contract to this project. Only he hadn't signed a piece of paper vowing silence under penalty of death, and he had a license to kill. For a moment he found it incredible no one bothered to mention the land south was choked with Indian reservations, and Jenkins couldn't help but wonder how long it would take before some rancher and his family fell deathly ill. Or how many other such experiments had already taken place, either here or across the borders in Utah or New Mexico.

The way he understood it, lethal doses of radiation exposure burned up the linings of the intestines, the brain, the muscle cells, a slow form of incineration from the inside out. Unless his fear and paranoia were inflaming his imagination right then, he would have sworn there was a yellowish-white halo shrouding the carcasses. Or was it simply the combined beams of roving flashlights casting an illusion before his eyes? Whatever, he turned his stare from both the living and the dead before his fear ran away with him. He fought some uncontrollable impulse to use the subgun.

Those slabs of prime beef would never see a rich man's dinner table, their problems over, but he knew lower levels of exposure often meant a malingering agony, what he'd come to think of as a fate worse than death. Having caught bits and snatches of their geek-babble during the day, he'd come to hear how 150 to 250 rads induced steady nausea and vomiting. Start climbing toward four and five hundred rads, cancer was a week or so away from grim genesis. Bone cells were bombarded, and bone marrows, which produced new blood cells, were all but clogged up by gamma and neutron poison. Lower resistance to all kinds of disease followed, slaughtering of the gene pool all but guaranteed, future generations of the unborn—if there ever would be such a thing—altered or...mutated into what? he wondered. Then there were radiation-induced abortions from chromosomal damage....

He shut down the line of ominous thought. They might as well have been speaking Martian, and still were.

"You guys ever speak in plain English?"

Timson swiveled his bubble head, and Jenkins caught the flicker of disdain shot his way. "Very well. Rad is a measure of radiation energy absorbed. Roentgen is a measure of radiation energy. Therefore one hundred roens creates one hundred rads and one hundred rems. Now the device pumped out over six hundred rads here—"

"Enough already. The damn thing works. Can we shut it down now?"

"It isn't enough that it works, Mr. Jenkins," Smith admonished. "We know plutonium can be burned to produce radioactive plutonium oxide particles. The amount we burned in the mini-incinerator of the, uh, device, as you call it, was less than half a kilo. Here's the math we computed. Four kilos burned for any length of time will provide lethal doses to a population of a quarter million. Our military principals want us to factor in weather conditions, natural barriers, radius typical to—"

"Shut it down!"

Whether it was his tone, look or the slight lift of the subgun he managed to freeze them cold, rewarded by a blessed moment of silence. Timson grumbled, but gave the order to turn the thing off. It was a wrap.

When Jenkins began trailing them up the gorge, angling away from the group, Smith found it necessary—whether to calm his fears or show off his pearls of geekdom—to prattle in his ear.

"You see, Mr. Jenkins, radiation lives in four forms. Alpha and beta, as far as this project goes and in terms of military significance, are of little or no value. Now gamma and neutron, which we have created, are highly penetrative...."

There it was. Jenkins stepped as lively as possible, throwing on his flashlight, searching out a swift course over the rock-strewn floor to clear him ever farther away from it. All things considered, it didn't look like much. Two parts, one about the size of a bedroom dresser, and the incinerator coupling, as they called it, no larger than a steamer trunk. Four vents to breath out the poison, a vertical computer panel to punch in the access codes hidden in a compartment on the thing's face.

The geek was babbling about pulsating pusher plates, and Jenkins tuned him out.

The frequency suddenly changed to his kind of people.

"Blackbird One to Z-Core Alpha, come in, Z-Core Alpha."

Jenkins keyed the button on his helmet, tying himself alone into his flyboy frequency. "Z-Core Alpha here. Go."

"I've got a sheep wandered onto the show, sir," the pilot told him, "sheep" being code for civilian. "Northeast ridge, Quad Six. My hot screens are turning up only one sheep, sir, hunkered down in a gulley."

Jenkins bit off a curse. He knew what had to be done, and there was no choice. It was time to go earn that blank check his strange savior from so long ago had handed over to him.

"Back off, Blackbird One, but maintain surveillance from a distance. If the sheep rabbits, track and shadow. Give me twenty minutes to decon then pick me up."

PRISON COU»LD MAKE or break a man, or so all of Vern Feller's ex-con buddies used to tell him around the pool table over beer and whiskey. Stretched out on the ridge on his belly, all those tales of prison life, visions of tattooed Jack Daniel's-slugging rednecks going through their macho posturing, bragging about kicking ass and taking names as they heroically fought off gang rape and murder attempts by the brothers and the greasers...well, all that sounded like pure bullshit in recall right then.

At least compared to what he now bore witness to.

His third full day on the run since robbing that liquor store in Abilene, gunning down the clerk in cold blood, then hot-wiring the old Chevy pickup out back, and

Vern Feller felt as if he were suddenly hiding out on the dark side of some distant unknown planet, light-years removed from anything real or even believable. His first night in the ancient ramshackle ruins of some mining ghost town, maybe a good mile north, and he'd ventured out with the .38 tucked in his waistband, 12-gauge sawed-off leading the way, when he'd first heard the godawful whapping of chopper blades. He set off, poised but quaking in terror, expecting the sky to open up and shower down with armed Feds. The stolen truck was hidden well enough in a cave beyond the rat-infested saloon where he'd taken up residence, but he was still certain the cops had found him.

If those stories about the big house were true, he decided he was neither willing, nor maybe man enough, he feared, to find out firsthand.

Somehow, he'd again found the stomach to take a look into the canyon beyond the rocky hills where the choppers seemed to confine their search. And once more came to discover figures in spacesuits, one of them armed with a submachine gun, while four spacemen toyed with some box in the canyon. Far to the west end it looked as if the same bunch of cattle were penned up, only tonight they were laid out, unmoving. But why?

A wave of nausea boiled up from his guts, and despite the chill in the air he was sweating as if he were baking under a noonday desert sun. What the hell were they doing down there? And why did he all of a sudden feel sick and weak? Fear of the unknown, it was that simple, he decided, terror sparked by images of the steel door slammed shut in his face to a waiting pack of hyenas.

This was too much. Dammit, all he wanted was to

make his way to San Francisco where an old girlfriend had just tossed out her live-in squeeze, told him, before he went postal in the liquor store, he was welcome back. He hadn't much cared if she was just rebounding, lonely, whatever. All he had known after putting the phone down was he needed quick cash, a change waiting in the wings, something, anything to get him out of shoveling shit in Abilene. Of course, freeing himself from child payments to an ex-wife who gouged up his check had served as motivation enough to get on the road and put Texas behind as just another bad lesson in lack of hormonal self-control.

Again he felt the urge to vomit, the bile squeezing up his chest like some fiery clenched fist, when the black helicopter soared his way. He burrowed deeper into the hole as the light wandered over the ridge. Did they know he had been watching the spaceman show for a good thirty minutes? Had they spotted him? Instinct told him they weren't cops, but at least one of them was armed, and that was reason enough for him to clear out of the ghost town just as soon as the chopper passed over him.

Discovery, much less getting cornered and captured, wasn't an option. And the state of Texas was famous for its insatiable appetite to clear them off Death Row.

It seemed like an hour before the white light turned away from the ridge and he was up and moving. On the run, Vern Feller's thoughts were focused on only the need to make the vehicle and put Colorado behind. Flight, survival, stay at large and off the Row. He'd been through too much, he decided, to never see the city by the Bay, secure the promise of a new life.

JENKINS WAS first off the chopper, leading the charge for what he assumed was the saloon, subgun up and tracking. Their lone sheep had been pegged on heat and infrared screens beating a hard course straight for some point beyond the bat-wing doors. Orders handed out on the flight in, his men were already securing a perimeter. And his role in the project had long since been defined. Any threat of discovery, even if it was some teenager out for a nature hike, was to be eliminated.

No witnesses, he thought, to the coming glory of the project, whatever that was.

He hit the boardwalk running, crouched and hugged the wall on one side of the bat wings while a two-man team took up position directly across, on the other side.

"Give it up!" Jenkins called, grateful to be free of the spacesuit, feeling light on his feet as he was propelled by adrenaline to wrap up this piece of dirty work. "You're surrounded!"

Jenkins nailed down the direction where the sheep was in hiding, the guy's voice bellowing in fear. "Up yours! I ain't going to prison! Come through those bat wings, and I'll start blasting!"

The sheep was armed, but Jenkins already knew that from first reports about the shotgun spotted by his flyboy when the guy broke from the ridge. They had a fugitive on the run, some loser, most likely, no one would miss. The sheep just happened to pick the wrong place and the wrong time to hole up and figure out his next move.

"We're not cops! We don't give a damn what you've done! Just throw down the weapon! We just want to talk!"

"No way! I'm walking out of here."

"I don't have time for this," Jenkins snarled in a quiet voice at his commandos, giving them the nod, holding up five fingers, indicating countdown, then began folding them one by one.

And went in first, low and surging on, peeling off to the side and holding back the trigger on his HK MP-5. The sheep caved to his panic, blasted off with the double barrels, but Jenkins was already scoring flesh, drilling the first few 9 mm projectiles through his mark's guts, homed in on the double flash and the sense-jarring sound of fury across the room. Two more subguns joined his barrage, the triburst carving the sheep into a dark mass of jerking human flesh.

The sheep went down for the slaughter. It was all easy enough, Jenkins thought, as he led his commandos deeper into the saloon, but they were pros with proven track records, not some armed punk crapping himself about the prospect of doing hard time.

Jenkins snapped on the flashlight taped beneath the subgun's muzzle, fanned it around the hellhole of cobwebs and rotting wood. His com link crackled, and he was informed about the truck, ski mask found under the seat. The sheep had not only been desperate and alone, but he'd been stupid, leaving evidence of a robbery laying around for anybody with common sense enough to put two and two together. Jenkins didn't care who the sheep was or what he'd done. Mission accomplished, he passed on the word to have the body dumped into the truck, the whole works to be put to the cleansing touch of their flamethrower.

1

Peace of mind.

Most likely this was a concept as illusive as peace on Earth in the lives of nearly all men, women and these days perhaps even the children in a post-Columbine America. In the world of Mack Bolan this nirvanaesque free-floating of the soul, where all was right and rosy, would have been like grabbing and holding on to a wisp of smoke. And standing down between missions was something as short-lived and apt to abrupt change as good weather.

"I'm Poe—that's with an *e*."

Bolan saw the shadow man waiting right where Hal Brognola informed him earlier he could be found for the midnight meet. The soldier proceeded with caution, angling away from his sedan rental vehicle, checking the gloom around the swing sets and slide, the empty ball field beyond, before he eased into the darker bowels of silent night on the outskirts of the park. Close enough to the Arlington Courthouse and Police Station—and at this witching hour—it wouldn't be a stretch to encounter a roving patrol car coming off Wilson Boulevard, cop wondering why two men were alone, in the dark, having a face-to-face about something, the discerning lawman's eye capable of reading the bulges under their coats for what they were.

Cops were exempt from Bolan's killing touch.

Beneath the Executioner's black windbreaker, the Beretta 93-R was nestled in its shoulder rigging, the big Israeli-made .44 Magnum Desert Eagle riding on his hip. In the event Bolan was dropped, badly wounded by a bullet and clinging to life, and an enemy moved in for the up-close and personal finish, a commando dagger was sheathed just above his ankle. Goring an adversary's family jewels or going for disembowelment with the razor-edged blade would definitely prove the last resort, but the whole setup felt out-of-kilter to Bolan, and he was braced for any surprises.

"Belasko," Bolan said, using his cover as Special Agent Mike Belasko of the Justice Department.

Brognola, who headed up Stony Man Farm's covert Sensitive Operations Group while twin billing as liaison to the President of the United States, had filled in Bolan best he could on what little he knew. Choppered from the Farm, Bolan had been greeted by the big Fed on the tarmac at Washington's Reagan National. Something about a black project involving a prototype military weapon of the nuclear variety. Rumors of the thing maybe getting put on the auction block to guys who didn't especially have the interests of a safe and secure America close to the heart. But, whenever he waded into spookdom, Bolan always found himself faced with more questions than answers, more lies than truth, more speculation than fact. And Brognola had handed off this one to the soldier with a shrug, a grimace and parting words of "Go meet the guy, hear what he has to say," before they split up for their respective vehicles.

Whatever lurked in the coming minutes, the Executioner wasn't a fan of mystery, just the same, and this little encounter had all the earmarks of a Chinese puzzle box.

Poe began confirming Bolan's suspicions the next moment.

"In certain circles some of us have come to refer to it as the Hellbox."

The soldier noted the large manila folder in Mr. Poe's hand, the bulge of a big handgun beneath his suit jacket. The mystery man could have been anywhere from forty to sixty, lean, in good shape, with eyes that might have told Bolan a hundred bad stories about a world gone mad, where the good guys did lose and the villains more often than not held the reins of real power, if the soldier was so inclined to ask. And Bolan skipped the usual inquiries, such as "what circles," who is "us." He trusted Brognola's instincts, the big Fed simply stating he'd caught some scuttlebutt about a potential problem from a reliable contact in the intelligence community who was willing to send a cutout, allegedly from the Pentagon's Fifth Ring, for a meet with Bolan to either look into it or walk away. Judgment call.

"You've got two minutes of my undivided attention," Bolan said.

Poe nodded, something Bolan couldn't nail down flickering through his eyes as he gave him the once-over. "I was told Mr. B. over at Justice is a man who gets things done. I was told a potential problem of this magnitude could get nipped in the bud, nailed down so hush-

hush in the realm of black ops it would be little more than just waking up trying to remember a bad dream."

"You're on the clock."

"Allow me some latitude here. Perhaps you know Congress sets aside a secret budget every year for so-called black projects, a number of which take place out in the southwest and western CONUS."

"I've heard the talk."

"Most of them involve prototype aircraft, government employees sworn to secrecy and under full working knowledge they can be terminated with extreme prejudice if they so much as flap a loose tongue after a few belts of booze at the local happy hour or pillow talk to their spouses with Big Brother, of course, having the bug in the feathers to catch it all."

"Old news."

"Well, here's something new. A blank check was handed over to FEMA by Congress roughly eighteen months ago. What do you know about the Federal Emergency Management Agency?"

"A lot more than I care to. Most people say they give disaster relief after a hurricane, flood, any area that's felt the wrath of Ma Nature. I know better."

Poe grunted. "Fact—Congress did a full investigation into FEMA after they were accused of dropping the ball following Hurricane Andrew. What they found was that FEMA was spending twelve times more for black projects—ostensibly preparing to aid and assist whoever survived the day after Armageddon—than they were for disaster relief programs. Fact—less than ten percent of the twenty-six hundred bureaucrats at FEMA were assigned to natural calamity duty. On the surface they appear typical government-issue clowns. Take off the mask, and you've got wolves in sheep's clothing who wield something close to the power of the Almighty."

Bolan turned on the wry charm. "I never have much spare time to catch the 'X-Files.'"

"The truth, as they say, Belasko, is always stranger than even some fiction a pampered Hollywood elite can conjure up. The truth, or part of it here, is this all goes beyond FEMA, all the way to the United States Army, even the Department of Defense, ending only God knows where. Groundwork, we believe, has long since been laid to ratchet up the heat in certain flashpoints around the world, reasons for which I cannot state with one-hundred percent certainty at this time. I see you—Mr. Cynical. No, sir, I haven't been watching too much Oliver Stone."

Bolan already knew some of what Poe told him. He'd had an up-close and personal encounter with a faction within FEMA. Also it seemed Aaron Kurtzman, cyber sorcerer at the Farm, had embarked on a new hobby whenever the Stony Man warriors were out of harm's way, meaning they were standing down or soaking up brief spells of R and R. He had created software he'd dubbed Follow the Black Helicopter. Essentially, he'd created a hacker's Pandora's box by which he could dance at will through the mainframes of every alphabet soup agency in search of data on so-called black projects. To some degree, Kurtzman had thrown fuel onto the fire of Brognola's suspicion about this Hellbox. Seemed Kurtzman had intercepted some cyber-space communiqués between FEMA, the Department of Defense and the CIA about something called Project Opus Damocles and a certain "foreign interest." Kurtzman promised more to follow, and Bolan could be sure if there was anything worth sinking megabyte teeth into, Kurtzman would chomp down and not let go until the truth was torn from under the surface.

"What's been created," Poe continued, "is a device that could not only perhaps revolutionize, even accelerate the pace in the arena of nuclear proliferation, but has the potential to unleash the Apocalypse before anyone is even remotely aware of why tens, even hundreds of thousands of people are dropping like the proverbial fly."

Bolan gave a look off to his flanks.

"We're alone, Belasko. I checked and double-checked my own six before meeting you. Truth is, what I'm divulging here could have me see some untimely accident. Looking at you, I'm sure that kind of risk is nothing new."

Bolan simply said, "I'm listening."

"Our side has invented a device that can create Chernobyl without something in the way of Hiroshima going off."

"Manufacture the fallout without the big bang."

"Exactly. Bottom line, and don't even ask me how the thing works, it creates and emits waves of radiation." He paused as if to allow the dramatic revelation to sink in. "Can you see the horror show unfolding here?"

Bolan could and did. If such a weapon existed the nightmarish possibilities were endless. Poe forged on, as if he was clairvoyantly one step ahead of the soldier's grim train of thought.

"That's right. A silent, invisible killer, a mass-mur-

dering ghost. Maybe smuggled into a city. Maybe
dropped by parachute to a countryside where the airspace isn't all that well monitored. Maybe set up behind
whatever is currently defined as a flashpoint or enemy
lines. Punch in the PALs—Permissive Action Links—
turn up the dial and pump out lethal levels of, say, six,
even seven hundred rems, and you've got whole seg-
ments of a potentially conquered populace, including
soldiers, cops, a guy like you or me, too damn sick and
weak, dying, in fact, to be bothered holding back the
march of armed spacesuits coming to grab up everything you cherish. In the hands of some terrorist, you
could hold a small country hostage, everything and
everyone contaminated by radiation. I'm told it doesn't
look like much more than your average bedroom dresser
set, something like a trunk fixed to the main housing.
But the old cliché about appearances..." He made a
point of checking his watch. "I see I've been allowed
overtime. You want more, or do you want to walk?"

"I'm still here."

"I'm prepared to hand over this package with the particulars as they're known. I'm prepared to steer you toward
an agent who is monitoring a certain situation out west."

"But?"

Poe looked away from Bolan, thinking about something. "I'll spare you the old cliché that if I told you..."

"I appreciate that."

"Yeah. You're not convinced this thing exists."

"Let's say it does. How many of these Hellboxes
are out there?"

"We've looked into it. We can't say. But from what

we've learned, once the kinks get worked out—and we believe they already have been—we might see a virtual factory-type assembly line, mass production in the near future of this thing, easy as making a watch or next year's automobile. Along the way, we might see a few of these things suddenly getting lost. You see the problem?"

"You're getting there."

"Another angle to think about. For some time now, a covert recruitment program has been in operation. Ask me exactly who the recruiters are, well, I can maybe hand over names, but nailing down who they answer to is another matter altogether. And forget about identifying those at the top of the feeding chain."

The guy was talking a lot but saying little, and Bolan found himself growing impatient. "Get to it."

"It's called Z-Core. They're a covert unit ostensibly under the command and control of the DOD. It's comprised of soldiers, a few spooks, NSA, CIA, dropped out of the fold for whatever reason. Most of the military types went mercenary for awhile, some floundered about in 'marginal lifestyles.' A few landed in prison, dogs of war committing crimes against a sovereign state, a few dabbling in the usual, drugs, gunrunning. Only the word from the void on my end is they found themselves suddenly plucked out of prisons in Third World zoos where their version of a better tomorrow simply meant a paycheck and maintaining the status quo of their paymasters."

"The strong arm for this Hellbox operation."

"A rogue factor, Uncle Sam's own little Gestapo. As we speak, I can tell you a few of these storm troopers are presently sitting on two men, part of the brains behind the Hellbox, in two separate locations. One such genius, retired from the program, had relocated to the Ozarks in Missouri. Appeared he wanted to sound off about the project, write a book about it or some such nonsense, guy even had a gig lined up with Geraldo and Katie. While he was driving into town one morning, it seems his brakes wouldn't work and he ended up taking the final swan dive into a ravine. Then his whole family, the wife, two kids, just so happen to fall fatally ill, the medical examiner stamping his conclusion to cause of death as food poisoning due to contaminated hamburger. Dig deeper, and you find out the wife was a vegetarian."

Bolan knew he had a decision to make, Poe standing there and looking at him, waiting for the verdict. It wouldn't be the first time the soldier had gone up against some shadow or rogue element on the home team where the good guys had jumped over to the other side of the tracks. Truth was, almost without exception, every campaign Bolan undertook involved some degree of conspiracy. It always came down to the basics, in the end, though, with some ugly truth rooted out on the business end of the soldier's weapons. Diplomacy and cleaning up the wreckage were someone else's headaches.

"Are you in?"

"You'll know soon enough."

With some reluctance, Poe handed over the package. "Either way, I'll trust you to put some fire to this."

"I know the drill."

"Everything you need to get started is in there. The void will fill me in eventually on your decision."

The final solemn words seemed to suspend themselves in the air as the shadow man turned and walked off. Bolan held his ground in the dark, watching as Poe was swallowed by the night.

BLACKBIRD ONE DROPPED him off at the old man's doorstep. The demon bird lifted off as soon as his rubber-soled combat boots touched the hard-packed earth, then took to the black skies south, soaring over a no-man's wasteland of volcanic rock and barren plain. He watched the chopper as it streaked off over desolation they said was once a lush jungle home to the dinosaurs and then the mastodons. The long dead and forgotten, but fossils and clues to the past, buried out there, waiting for men quite unlike him, geeks like the nuke boy wonders who could maybe answer the big questions. He wondered why he tended to think the world was a better place when man didn't inhabit the Earth.

As the cloud of grit cleared and the whapping buzz was swallowed by the impenetrable blackness of the empty bowels of northeastern New Mexico, Burt Jenkins found himself pulling up short near the stoop. The black mobile home was nearly invisible, would have blended in as just another part of the desolation except for the soft white burn flickering beyond the single curtained window. The satellite dish, he noted, also black, jutted from the roof, with a series of optical cable wires spreading away from the dish like some steel spiderweb.

The man known as Raven was so hooked in to everything he needed to know he could play God from behind those walls, and did. Out here in the middle of the devil's guts, which pretty much defined the American Southwest as far as he was concerned, the entire cyber world—from NORAD and the NRO, to the CIA, NSA and the Fifth Ring—was one stroke of the man's fingers over a keyboard away.

Jenkins was never sure how he felt about the old man who had saved him from certain execution in countries most Westerners, he thought, couldn't even point to on the globe. There were moments, like now, when the ex-mercenary wasn't sure how he even felt about his own life. It was so quiet, so dark and still, Jenkins felt the weight of the past fall over him like some moldy shroud. It came to him without warning, some fiery point of anger knotting up his chest, forcing him to recall past images he had made a lifetime out of trying to run from and forget. One flashing moment he saw an orphaned little snot in his mind's eye, bounced from foster home to foster home or maybe dumped for a stretch into the laps of usually drunken feuding relatives. Then there was a young, angry vague shadow of yesteryear, marching into the Army recruitment center, a skinny whelp with a John Wayne complex, gung-ho about something he had only fantasized about. A naive kid, to be sure, having lost himself over the years in celluloid glorification of guys who'd probably never even been in a serious knuckle-duster where fists broke teeth and shattered bone and the other guys did kick you when you were down, but someone who was burdened with a soul that was damn sure painfully aware he had proved a failure up to then at everything he had attempted in life.

Sports, relationships, basic school studies—it ate up his guts like some cancer to recall that he couldn't even rank among the mediocre in the old civilian life, and forget about fitting in somewhere to prove to the world at large he had some merit in their eyes. Wet dreams were just that—wet and useless in real time. The problem, though, didn't end in the waning teenage years, and his search for adventure through combat never became the reality he craved in hopes of finding if he had the right stuff to stand out among ordinary men and get counted.

It happened later, discovering the tiger under the *F* for failure he imagined was carved like disfigurement on his face, when he was about as far removed from being a legitimate soldier as Pluto was to the Earth.

The old man, on the other hand, was some kind of decorated war hero, bona fide and recognized in every sense, imbued with the calm self-confidence that was merit enough in the eyes of peers or wannabes. Try as he might, Jenkins couldn't deny that was the separation between the two of them, the distance he endured, almost like some badge of shame he wore whenever he was in the man's presence, although the old man always spoke to him as if they were equals. To some extent that only seemed to make it worse, and he was always left wondering if he was being patronized. A small voice wanted to whisper from somewhere deep in the caverns of his head. Jenkins gritted his teeth to the point where he pumped the blood pressure into his ears. Unsure what he resented most—the past or the guy beyond the door—he tried but failed to blank out the thought that this old man was really the father he'd been looking for, or angry with, all his life.

Which was one reason he'd allowed himself to get drawn into the web of the project, willing to walk in the shadows of someone else's glory.

Squaring his shoulders, Jenkins marched up the stoop, opened the door and moved into what he thought of as God's lair. Closing the door with a quiet snick, he found the old man in his small rolling chair, sitting like a piece of that volcanic stone beyond the walls, inside his horseshoe desk.

"I understand the situation has been sanitized," the old man said without looking up from the screen of his laptop.

"Yes, sir. We ran a background. The civilian was wanted for armed robbery and the murder of a liquor-store clerk."

"Sounds like something of a cosmic justice to me."

Jenkins felt himself go rigid in the man's presence, standing at attention as he usually did, then the wizened face turned his way from out of the dancing shadows of the scrolling screen. The former mercenary might have thought of him as the old man, but he had one of those ageless faces despite the full head of white hair, the crow's feet around the blue eyes, the hint of a sagging jowl. Timeless and wise.

King Solomon.

And Jenkins rarely saw him without a glass of whiskey, neat, or a cigar burning smoke to hover some around-the-clock halo over his head. He had to have had the constitution of...what? A white shark? Assault the body with poison, but ever-moving, never slowing, never showing the first clue the brain was maybe on the verge of getting pickled?

"Care for a drink, son?"

Jenkins hesitated, willing off a sudden flare of anger at what sounded almost like some aloof intimation or perceived dig at the differences between them. He rarely indulged alcohol on the job anyway, believing anything that affected the senses—sometimes even putting sex in that category—could dull the fighting edge when he might need it most. But the voice came back, urging him to go on, that the bridge between them was perhaps no longer that far. If nothing else, shedding blood was the one bond they shared.

"Yes, sir, I believe I will. Thank you."

"Help yourself then."

The small wet bar was planted next to the giant-screen television. The sound was off, an old black-and-white war movie leaping out at Jenkins from the screen as he went and built a whiskey on the rocks.

"It's incredible, you know that."

"What is, sir?" Jenkins sipped his drink, took several steps across the Spartanly furnished living room.

The old man stared at the computer screen. "What they've created. I heard somewhere our nation's nuclear arsenal equals seven thousand billion pounds of TNT. I did some computing here, and given the present population of the world, that's about ten pounds of one radioactive explosive per pound of each singular man, woman and child on the planet. My point is that if they can mass-produce the box, our side may never have to worry about the other side ever launching a few ICBMs. A neat, clean step into mankind's future. We can effectively neutralize the opposition. Conquer and divide without the loss of one soldier. Only we both know there's always been another agenda."

And there it was, Jenkins thought, the bottom line.

"You're referring, of course, sir, to our foreign interest," he said, and wondered why he had always been kept in the dark where the identity of what was sometimes also referred to as "the client" was concerned.

"One reason I've called you here. It's, also, as I'm sure you've always suspected, why I paid to get you out of prison in both countries."

"Can I ask you something?"

"By all means."

"Was I intended to eventually become a sacrificial lamb in some...grand plan?"

"No. But we are all expendable, it's simply a question of one's personal priorities and one's ability to make it happen. Being the instrument of your freedom had another, I suppose you might say noble, perhaps even somewhat sentimental reason.... Ancient history."

He seemed to dwell on something, a dark expression shadowing his face. "You know what I saw in you, Burt?" Another pause, the old man sipping whiskey, working on his cigar, a look in his eyes that made Jenkins feel as if he were being both measured and viewed in a new light. "I saw drive, determination, character. I saw the makings of a warrior, the old-school kind, mired, even lost, however, a diamond in the rough, a T-Rex in a new age where honor is nothing more these days than a word in Webster's. Part of the problem with the world today, especially in this country, we're made to believe failure is something akin to suicide. You don't finish first the first time out of the gate, they look at you funny, a pariah, if they even bother to look at you at all. Sometimes effort and guts alone are reward enough. History is full of great or infamous men, depending on your view, who tried and failed at many things in their lives before they found their calling as warriors."

Jenkins wasn't sure he cared for the implication but said, "I've always been grateful to you."

"I know."

Jenkins spotted the smaller monitors from his standpoint. They shone back, a greenish glow detailing the craggy grounds surrounding the mobile home. He slugged back the whiskey, unable to help wondering what the old man had thought—if anything—when he had stood at his front door, chewing on his own thoughts and somewhat fucked-up feelings.

"Things are about to go hot," the old man said, and Jenkins believed he saw something like a dark veil fall over the expression of his benefactor. "I have caught some rumblings from the void. Trouble could be headed our way."

"Sir?"

"I'm going to call back our ride. We're going relocate this command center closer to home base."

Jenkins understood the logistics but didn't grasp the full implications. He knew the mobile base could be lifted by steel winches fixed to one of the Blackbirds. Home base was the classified, heavily guarded labyrinth dug into the mountains to the south. The old man moved his command center around by chopper as easily as he might drive one of the black SUVs into the nearest town. What disturbed Jenkins were the blanks about this trouble.

"We'll discuss it further on the way," the old man said, and shut down the laptop. "I've filled you in, strictly need-to-know, up to this point. From here on, things are about to change. Understand something, and let us be crystal clear. From the beginning, before I even laid eyes on you, there were those—myself included—who would be the ones at the helm of inventing a new future, at least in terms of the nuclear one, or at the very other end of the ominous spectrum, a total abolishment of the day for the human race through another avenue. So I ask you now. Are you willing to do whatever is necessary, are you willing to carry out orders even if, deep inside, you may have grave doubts?"

Despite the sudden freeze in his belly, Jenkins managed to keep the fear off his face. "I owe you my life, sir. I consider myself a soldier. I will do whatever it is you ask."

Was that the ghost of an approving smile? Now that a gloomier murk was cast over the old man's face, Jenkins couldn't be sure. Not that it mattered. It was enough, in his mind, at least, that he was being trusted, called upon even, the old warrior believing him capable of the ultimate sacrifice if needed.

"Then it's settled," the old man said. "But I'm not going to bullshit myself or you. I see you, and I know you demand more out of life than a blank check from the void that would land you on easy street. I've walked down easy street, son. I'm here to tell you, it's not for men like us."

Jenkins could believe that, or wanted to, as a warm flush of pride washed over him.

The Executioner's mystery tour was roughly underway by a good hour after the jet touched down, when the hint of a dirty predawn golden shade began to spread over the barren scrubland of central New Mexico. Fisting the wheel of his SUV rental, the soldier read the posted sign that stated he was a handful of miles and counting to Santa Rosa. Only meet number two would take place at a diner on the western fringes of Santa Rosa proper, near the junction of Highway 54 and I-40. During the flight to Albuquerque, the soldier had touched base via a scrambled line—prior arrangements courtesy of Mr. Poe—to the contact of the hour. They settled on the rendezvous point, complete with ETA and the obligatory password.

Interstate 40 was the main artery through New Mexico, but other than a semi, a few vehicles with out-of-state tags and a lone highway patrol cruiser heading the opposite way, west, Bolan had the road to himself at that gloomy hour. Even still, despite the noticeable lack of human beings, the soldier maintained his watch on the highway, beyond and ahead, while clipping along at a smooth sixty-five mph. And, as of yet, no black helicopters were roving the skies above the desolation beyond the highway. But the classified base in question was, allegedly, a little too far east and north to warrant the burning up of fuel for any black-suited flyboys to bother extending—whatever their paranoia—this far west.

Not that the soldier would be surprised if an undetermined threat reared up out of nowhere. Bolan had been down the black project route before, and he'd come to expect the unexpected, braced once again for the worst. From previous almost deadly experience when dealing with the shadow men who ran the most ominous of classified games, he suspected that before it was over—if the threat of some conspiracy was real and a rogue factor was looking to unload this Hellbox to a foreign enemy of the U.S.—he'd find himself in a dark world where nothing was what it appeared to be. He'd seen their kind before, so-called agents for the home team who could talk a convincing Stars-and-Stripes, National Security game out of both sides of the mouth while planning his sudden demise and sticking it to the powers who had placed them in charge of a black project. Traitors who went for themselves, whether out of greed, warped ideology, disillusionment with the status quo or simple lust for power, if it played out to his own previous bad experience Bolan could count on encountering the worst kind of savage. They were men who were pretty much—at least in their own eyes—given the power to play God, sanctioned all the way, just the same, by Uncle Sam to turn up the notch in creating prototype and ultrasecret instruments of war. The power of their black budgets permitted them to spare no expense, and their license to kill allowed them to silence loose tongues that might flap wild tales to anyone who would listen, help get the ball rolling about government conspiracies, secret planning of Armageddon, chemical experiments on unsuspecting civilians, light shows in the night skies believed to be either UFOs or prototype aircraft black-engineered by government sorcerers with more clearance and clout than the President of the United States.

Separating truth from fantasy or the fantastic wasn't a problem for Bolan, since he was interested in the facts only. And he knew enough about what went on out here in the Southwest to get the gist of the picture. Even still, whether they came from the bowels of mountain bases in the form of high-tech super aircraft or new angles for the dispersal of germ, chemical or nuclear agents, created either for offensive or defensive purposes, the men in charge of such projects were authorized with the ultimate power to use deadly force even on unsuspecting civilians.

Especially on civilian trespassers. And even a badge from the Justice Department, bogus as it was in Bolan's case, meant about as much of an irritant to these men as a fly picking the scabs on the back of a water buffalo.

Which put Bolan in a strange new world, going up against agents of the government, where he might be forced to make a judgment call on the spot in regards to meeting such force the only way he knew how to save his own skin. Blessed by Uncle Sam or not, they were fair game on Bolan's menu if they wanted to go on the muscle or beyond.

Bolan gave a search of no-man's-land but found only a vacant brown landscape.

A weary traveler might have begun daydreaming at this point, yearning for the snow-blanketed ski slopes of some mountain resort or white sandy beaches of a tropic paradise where the rum flowed and the bikinis stretched all around. Anyplace, in fact, imagined in the mind that would help blot out the sweeping nothingness between Albuquerque and his destination.

The Executioner, though, could ill afford the luxury of fantasy.

The flight and the drive had lent Bolan ample time to rehash the situation, given the few details Mr. Poe had provided. Following his departure from Poe, the soldier had touched base with Brognola who had gone to work laying the foundation for basic logistics to get him to something of a launch point for an undefined mission. Two items—a wristwatch-type Geiger counter and a hazardous material biosuit—were delivered to Bolan with all the promptness he'd come to expect from the big Fed. His war bag was already aboard the waiting Gulfstream jet, the soldier rarely leaving home—Stony Man Farm—without the necessities to tackle a campaign. He kept it simple for this outing, an M-16 with attached M-203 grenade launcher, a mini-Uzi that could be threaded with a sound suppressor, spare clips all around. Then there was a mixed bag of grenades, both the handheld kind and 40 mm projectiles to feed the M-203 in the event it was needed to even the odds. Satlink with fax, of course, in the bag, and a cell phone with scrambled line clipped to his belt. There was a skintight blacksuit and a combat harness housed in the big nylon bag. All told, he figured, it was enough to get it started. The second bag housed his biosuit, but he hoped it didn't come down to some armed jaunt in a radioactive hotbed.

But what, exactly, was he expected to uncover out here? Tackle what, and take on whom? Before flying from D.C. he told himself he'd give it twenty-four hours. If no threat to national security was rooted out, then the soldier would leave the state in peace to all its spookdom, UFO buffs and doomsayers.

A few more miles, getting out of his head, aware only time, some Q and A and perhaps a soft probe of this mysterious base, and Bolan found the diner off Highway 54, tucked in a tourist strip of motels and fast food joints. Pulling into the lot, he noted the Jeep Cherokee he'd already been informed would be there to announce the presence of his contact. And it was fitted with government plates. The agent who called himself Rockwell, Bolan thought, wasn't big on the subtle touch. Was it arrogance, negligence or something else? Rockwell broadcasting his affiliation with the government didn't boost the soldier's confidence in the man. Seasoned pros, whether soldiers or spies, didn't announce themselves to anyone who might pose more than a passing curiosity or a threat to their own well-being.

The soldier slipped in between a Harley-Davidson motorcycle and a vintage red Ford pickup. A moment later, the engine shut off, and Bolan was out the door, his dark windbreaker a size too big concealing his standard side arms well enough to pass fleeting scrutiny.

He was making his way toward the front door, giving his rear a last look, when the soldier saw the black four-door sedan pulling into the lot. The Executioner looked away, but he'd made out at least three shadows behind the tinted windshield. Radar for trouble mentally blipping in his head, Bolan sensed their watching eyes as he opened the door and moved inside for his meet with Mr. Rockwell. The sun wasn't even up yet, and already something warned the Executioner the new day was set to turn hot.

"ALLOW THEM their powwow, then approach and proceed. When it's done I will send out a cleanup crew. Out."

Jenkins looked away from the old man, aware something was set to go down on the other side of Santa Rosa. He'd seen that look in the old man's eyes before, a cold glittering that seemed to spark from some hidden knowledge behind the eyes whenever he passed on orders that spelled out termination.

Jenkins went back to staring down the lot, figuring the old man would fill him in at some point when he was good and ready. The motel they had under watch was planted on the east end of Santa Rosa among a string of cheap dives, greasy spoons, a hodgepodge of typical scenery, Jenkins thought, that greeted the truckers and family-oriented travelers who needed a break from the grim vacancy of the drive between the Texas border with New Mexico and this next outpost of anything close to civilization beyond Tucumcari to the east.

The chopper ride to base had been swift enough. A black SUV had been waiting for Jenkins to take the wheel and drive the old man to the site where he clearly had something lethal waiting in the wings. Whatever the goal here, the old man had kept it to himself, but Jenkins had faced this sort of setup before, where the old man sat in stony quiet for a long spell before laying out the plan. All Jenkins knew was that a two-man team from his Z-Core had been posted here to baby-sit one of the brains behind the Hellbox. An hour ago, a Lincoln Town Car had pulled up in front of the door to the room they'd been watching. Four swarthy types in suit jackets, one lugging a briefcase, had disgorged from the luxury vehicle and marched inside, leaving Jenkins with still more questions hanging.

"Listen carefully," the old man suddenly said. "Our four friends in the Lincoln are from the Pakistani ISI."

Jenkins kept his expression neutral as he watched the old man watching the door to the room in question. The ISI, he knew, was Pakistan's rough equivalent of the CIA, begging still more questions Jenkins most likely wouldn't get answered anytime soon.

"At this time, all you need to know is you let me do the talking once we go in." The old man turned, and Jenkins felt the piercing look even if his eyes were obscured by the dark sunglasses. "Fix your side arm with your sound suppressor. We go in as soon as I hear back about our new guest from the east."

IT WASN'T the best place to conduct a line of questioning about national security and military conspiracies, complete privacy dubious, hinging on a couple of factors. At least his contact in the predescribed flaming aloha shirt had taken a booth at the deep end of the diner, near a jukebox that was pulsing a country tune. A sweeping look around, and Bolan read what appeared somber satisfaction on the faces of the few patrons at that early-morning hour over the choice of tunes. There was enough space between his contact's perch and the nearest pair of potential eavesdropping ears—a biker donning Hell's Angels colors at the counter—to give Bolan a chance to fire off some Q and A in relative security.

All things being relative, though, Bolan believed some undetermined risk was heightened by the occupants of the sedan. A look to the side, and he found the sedan was creeping along beyond the plate-glass window, coming to rest behind his SUV.

Not good.

Mr. Aloha looked up from the menu, dark shades hiding the eyes and keeping Bolan from gauging whatever might be churning in his head. The lean buzz-cut guy in black jacket and slacks had occupied the last booth, back to the wall. That would be the first change in the program if Bolan decided to take a seat. The bulge his contact sported under the coat didn't escape Bolan's fleeting scrutiny either.

The contact was on the verge of blurting the password, something about steak and eggs, when Bolan threw a look over his shoulder, found no one paying them the least bit of attention, faced the guy and quietly growled, "Skip it. You were either followed or those are friends of yours in the sedan. Don't look."

The contact seemed ready to launch himself into an angry response, scowling, then the expression faded and he turned into Mr. Cool. "Okay. How about the former."

"How about you get up and give me your seat." The contact hesitated, and Bolan pushed. "Or I'm gone."

"I can see trust isn't part of your nature."

"If I'm getting set up or jerked around, you'll like other parts of my nature even less."

"That sounds fair enough."

Bolan slipped his hand inside the windbreaker, fisting the Beretta, angling himself between the contact and any watching eyes. A shake of his head, as if he couldn't believe they were getting off on the wrong foot, but the contact rose, squeezed past Bolan and dropped into the bull's-eye side of the booth.

"You're not what I expected," Rockwell said, sounding as if he hoped to measure Bolan with his next response.

Gaze narrowed, the soldier eased down into the booth, vigilant even with his back to the wall. Some sixth sense, perfected over the eternal years in the hell grounds, allowed him to see everything around him without having to look directly at it. Such as noting the sedan rolling away, slowly veering across the lot for 54.

"Let's start over," Bolan said. "The sedan."

Bolan spotted a dour waitress in gray beehive making her way toward the booth. He was already taking out the cash that made up his walking-around war funds, peeling off a ten and holding it up before she had a chance to take an order. "My friend and I aren't eating. Just a few minutes of privacy."

There was just enough edge in Bolan's tone to keep her quiet and compliant as she took the money, then made her way back to the counter. Bolan saw they were drawing a lingering eye from the biker, the one-percenter smoking up a storm but finally turning away to pull a small flask from his vest to spike his coffee with the morning's medicine.

"Whatever Poe handed over to you should have filled you in."

"He came up short," Bolan said. "My original question?"

Rockwell edged up, lowering his voice. "Let's just say these men, like the ones in the sedan, aren't prone to forsake their sworn duty."

"One last chance for straight talk."

"Bodyguards, assassins, executioners, take your pick. They're on to me. There, I said it. They're more than likely on a hunting expedition. On the other side of town, an armed detail is sitting on a man we know helped to create their toy. We have evidence this thing has been openly tested in Colorado and here in New Mexico without authorization from anyone back east. We have discovered that cases of thyroid cancer, just to name a few ills, have doubled out here in the past year. We believe the project called Opus Damocles has gone rogue."

"Who is we?"

"I work for a division of the NSA. Our specialty is the tracking and monitoring of black projects. I understand you were informed about one suspicious death. It wasn't the first. The problem now is that this rogue element is prepared to resort to a kidnapping of the families of two specialists they are presently sitting on."

"And you know all this how?"

"A man on the inside. Our suspected conspirators have plans to sell one, maybe more of these boxes overseas to an as yet undetermined buyer. We've narrowed it down to a few shoppers— terrorists or marginal intelligence operatives—in either Pakistan or Afghanistan. A Major Suhwan Boshab of the Pakistani ISI has been seen entering the motel room in question, we believe to put a down payment on a box. First in line, so to speak. The word I get is that potential buyers are more interested in dismantling the thing in hopes of grabbing up some weapons-grade plutonium. Further, I'm hearing how the specialists being sat on are also up for bids. The bottom line being they can help advance an ongoing or fledgling nuclear program or show some terrorist, who up to now has only blown up a bus in Tel Aviv maybe, how to create a nuclear explosion out of the box. Something primitive but relatively easy, if what I'm hearing is accurate. Say a trigger device, a gun type, like the one dropped on Hiroshima."

A dozen questions leaped to mind, but Bolan glanced out the window—in time to spot the sedan swinging into the lot.

"Your friends are back."

Shooting a look into the lot, Rockwell growled at Bolan, "You're either with me on this or you're not."

"Meaning I trust you."

"I'm sure you'll make some judgment call eventually on that score."

"I'm sure I will. Here it is. We take my vehicle out of here...."

"Hey, look, I'm not—"

"Give a little, get a little. That's the way it's going to be."

"Sounds like I'll be doing all the giving."

"I was counting on that being part of the arrangement. Right now, I'd be ready for anything if I were you."

The sedan moved beyond Bolan's line of sight, past the far edge of the diner. Unless he missed his guess a few human sharks were circling in for a back-door strike.

"Let's move. Lead the way," Bolan told his contact.

It was a quick dive inside his windbreaker, drawing then holding the Beretta low by his leg when no one was watching. Bolan rose, working grim vigilance between the swing doors to the kitchen behind the counter and the parking lot. He ignored the boozy glower from the biker, trailing Rockwell for the door, combat senses flaring to life.

Something in the way the sedan came back, boldly announcing itself again, circling the diner, out of sight, told Bolan it was ready to hit the fan.

It did.

Rockwell was marching for the SUV's passenger side, Bolan angling down the front, when the sedan whipped around the corner, off to the soldier's right. They came in hard and fast, the wheelman throwing the vehicle into a hard lurch, blocking the SUV in its slot. The Executioner was raising the Beretta when the wheelman and comrade burst out the doors, compact submachine guns flying up and cutting loose.

3

They got as far as they did simply because Bolan indulged a rare temptation to give them the benefit of the doubt. If the two men in black were, in fact, legitimate but classified operatives of the government, it stood to reason they'd either be foolish or blind insane to engage in a gunfight in full public view. The simple fact they came out firing implied two critical matters he wouldn't soon forget or forgive. First, the hit was ordered by someone higher up the food chain, desperate to hide something and keep a secret agenda rolling along. Second, these men and whatever clandestine group they belonged to believed they were above the law, and any threat, real or perceived, civilian or otherwise, was to be dealt with by the business end of their weapons. The desert was big and lonesome enough to hide a mere two bodies, after all. And what the scavengers didn't claim Mother Nature would dispose of.

That was assuming, of course, he included Rockwell on their menu for an intended body count.

The soldier was beating a hard course toward the nose of the red pickup when hot lead sailed past, the diner's rear stucco face tattooed with the thunk of steel-jacketed projectiles. The initial angle of attack the wheelman took, having slid the sedan too close for comfort to the SUV, forcing him to shoot over the roof in first hopes of a quick lucky score, gave Bolan an edge to counterattack. The shooter was close to seven feet tall, and it wasn't any leap in logic for him to pursue his original idea.

Classified Man One was sidling beyond the SUV's rear, realizing his first few rounds had flown wide, attempting to line up a better shot, when Bolan tapped the Beretta's trigger, shooting across his body. On the fly, firing up at an angle, it was quite the killshot, but Bolan hardly had the time to admire his grim work. Even still, he glimpsed the look of dumbfounded confusion that might have been comical under any other circumstances, the shooter's eyes bugging out as a ragged crimson hole blossomed in the center of his forehead. Long legs wilted like wet noodles and he dropped, taking that what-the-hell expression to the grave.

The barking handgun jolted Bolan's attention toward Rockwell, who was hunkered down behind the SUV's starboard nose. His contact was capping off rounds downrange with a 9 mm Glock, but the cracking of glass punched out and slivers tinkling off asphalt near the sedan told the Executioner the man was probably falling short of scoring flesh.

The stubby SMG was a distorted shadow through the side and back windows of the SUV, flaming away to confirm Bolan's suspicion that Classified Man Two was still alive and fighting mad. Crouched, Bolan charged the rear, flicked the selector mode to 3-round-burst mode and let the Beretta rip. Shooter Two saw it coming too late, his angry focus torn between Bolan and dodging the return fire from the other side of the SUV. He was in the act of ducking below the starboard fender when the triburst of 9 mm subsonic Parabellum manglers blew half his face off in a bloody wash while tunneling through his brain and puking out the side of his skull in a ragged tuft of meat and flying bone fragments.

There was another gunner, maybe two, somewhere, Bolan was sure of it.

And he came out the front door, opening up with the Ingram MAC-10 his dead pals had favored.

Rockwell hit the deck, the Harley's engine twanged by tracking lead but blocking off certain death, at least for the moment. Hurling himself across the rear end of his rental car, Rockwell pinned to cover, and Bolan came around the corner, the Beretta spewing a triburst that zipped Shooter Three across the chest, spinning him where he stood. Gravity took over after death claimed the cosmic workings of the inner man, and he dropped, crashing into the door, an arm spasm spearing an elbow through the glass facing.

Holding his turf for a stretched second, Bolan scanned the lot, both corners of the diner, the front door. Satisfied it was three up and three down, he dropped into the sedan, put it into drive and rolled it a few yards ahead. Flight cleared, he was frisking his second victim in dim hopes of finding some ID when Rockwell said, "Forget about it. These guys don't even have Social Security numbers."

Maybe not, Bolan thought, but he fished out a magnetic swipe card from the dead man's coat pocket. Sometimes, Bolan knew the fickle gods of covert war sent a cosmic gift horse his way. With no telling where it was all headed from here, the soldier would seize every bit of edge, stolen or otherwise, he could take.

The Executioner was moving, taking the SUV's wheel and firing up the engine, when the Hell's Angel shoved his weight into the door. Even over the roar of the SUV's engine Bolan heard the biker snarling curses as he banged his bulk into the door, knocking loose the corpse that had him wedged against the jamb.

Bolan reversed all the way across the lot on a scream of rubber clawing at the asphalt. He hit the brake and threw the wheel hard left, whipping the front end around to point toward Highway 54.

Bolan saw the Hell's Angel shrinking fast but shaking a fist his way in the side glass. But the Executioner had a bellyfull of ominous foreboding that some biker, stranded and pissed off about his shot-up hog, was the least of his problems.

IF HE CAUGHT the gist of the one-way conversation right, after the old man's contact with Alpha Two backup, the trouble from back east was headed their way. Alpha Two Force had initiated contact, as ordered, and been cashiered by one of two unknown hostiles for their effort in a firefight in front of a diner on the other side of town. Vague descriptions of the two shooters, but there was at the least a positive make on their sports utility vehicle. So the old man had passed off new orders, shifting tactics before they even went to work here, the play, it seemed, suddenly getting called by the nameless opposition.

So much for quick and easy.

The game took on a whole new dimension—the unknown adversary winning round one—and even before the sun had fully risen the coming day promised to either work on his nerves or send him soaring to new heights of battlefield glory. Pursue the SUV, which was right then cutting across Santa Rosa, eastbound, that was the standing order. Coming for their heads, at worst, or, at best, looking to challenge their authority? Engage them in some ultimate confrontation to unravel whatever the hopes and dreams of the project? Well, the old man would go to great lengths, he knew, to eliminate this problem before it snowballed and gained the momentum of an avalanche. Jenkins wasn't concerned about the prospect of being forced to deal with New Mexico officialdom or worry that the highway patrol would drop some dragnet, snaring them when they finally made their way to home base. The wheels had already been greased in that respect. Local cops, he knew, wouldn't even prove so much a nagging irritant, with their cordoned crime scenes and endless flurries of questions, since the old man had dispatched a cleanup crew from a motel on the west side of Santa Rosa. They were government agents, but a special task force of Z-Core that had long since been inserted as "sworn deputies." If some badge wanted to raise a stink just the same, Jenkins knew the old man could put in a quick call to the Pentagon where their watchdog from the Fifth Ring would claim sanction by executive order from the President, thus sending some irate lawman skulking off and muttering to himself. Smoke screen, of course, the umbrella of presidential blessing, since not even the Chief Executive had the first clue Opus Damocles existed. "I need this wrapped up, son, two minutes and counting. You'll see to it you take care of the clown watching us on the way out."

Jenkins didn't need to look down the lot to know the black sedan with government plates had them under surveillance. An earlier computer check of the plates turned up nothing, the numbers, in fact, vanishing altogether in cyber space. The CIA didn't weave their spook webs on U.S. soil. So that left the NSA, DIA and a half dozen other possible agencies. For damn sure, someone was digging around in their business, but just how much did they know or suspect? Fact was the old man had stated he knew the guy had been there, watching the room the whole night. The G-man's partner, according to what little he'd gleaned from Raven, was one of the two shooters from the diner. So who was the other guy, the one from back east, allegedly doing all the killing? Boring ahead, gun blazing, from the bits and snatches he'd caught from the old man, some big guy shooting up his own professional soldiers...like what? Like he'd been there before? Was one of them?

Whatever, the ex-merc's own order was clear, but Jenkins knew it would wait until the dirty work inside the motel room was concluded.

There was no need to knock, since they were both expected, so Jenkins trailed the old man into the room and shut the door. It was spacious enough to hold all of them, he saw, with some degree of comfort to spare. Which meant plenty of elbow room to allow quick clearance of his own weapon, none of their targets able to make a grab for his gun once the shooting started.

The old man got down to business. He nodded at the briefcase in the ISI major's hand. "The money?"

Jenkins eased two steps away from the old man and edged toward the wall, his back to the curtained window. The setup looked easy enough, and going through with the butcher work here should go off without a hitch, once, of course, he factored in the element of ruthless surprise. On the far side of the bed two of his Z-core soldiers, Block and Jocarto, watched the Pakistanis, his men with their hands clasped over their groins, dark shades maybe hiding their eyes but Jenkins reading the tension etched on their faces, his guys anticipating the moment of grim truth. On their part, the Pakistanis held their own piece of turf, a staggered line near the dresser off to his right. Easy. The problem, though, could prove the master geek he knew as Charles Timbers. Fear and anger right then fought for control of the specialist's gaunt and haggard face as he worked a look, bordering on outrage, around the room. The specialist started to rise from his seat by the dresser, but the old man stuck out a hand, some unspoken threat that sent Timbers sinking back in his chair. When it started, Jenkins couldn't help but wonder if the specialist would muck up the whole play. Would the guy start screaming his head off? Bolt for the door, create some ungodly scene to bring any curious onlookers from other rooms who would, in turn, have to be dealt with?

Wait and see, Jenkins told himself.

Major Boshab cracked an ugly grin, showing a set of chipped brown teeth, then settled the briefcase on the bed before keying opened the two latches. Jenkins pictured a shark smiling before it chomped down on bleeding prey. The ISI man lifted the lid, holding out a hand as if to proudly announce his good faith on the deal. "Half a million, American. Another half when the device is trucked to the agreed-upon destination. Final payment once it is safely delivered to my country."

"There's been a change in plans," the old man said.

The shark's grin vanished, the hawkish face hardened by a dark scowl. "What change?"

"The deal's off. Someone made a better offer."

"What?"

The old man went for it next, the sound-suppressed Browning Hi-Power filling his hand as if it were some magic trick. The coughing retort was louder than Jenkins might have cared for, in case the crashing of bodies jolted some occupants in the adjacent rooms and sent them dialing the office, but the old man had made the call already to commit, do it and walk away. No stopping, no turning back, and any witnesses or squawking mouths would be silenced on the way out. Whatever questions Jenkins wanted to pose were on hold.

It was slaughter time.

The old man shot Boshab point-blank in the face. At that range, the muffled blast and muzzle velocity knocked the ISI major off his feet as if some black belt in karate had leg-swept him at the ankles. In his experience, though, Jenkins knew killing a man, even in cold blood with the edge of shock on his side, was never as easy as they made it look out in Hollywood where Sly and Bruce and Arnold could waste half a herd of bad guys in one clip, not even blink. No one really wanted to die, he briefly thought, not even the coward or the wannabe suicide. Even someone unaccustomed to violence would somehow fight to cling to their last moment on Earth, pursuing avenues of attack or escape—fueled and elevated to nearly superhuman heights by pure fear and adrenaline—that they would have never imagined themselves capable of.

The three standing Pakistanis proved Jenkins's past experience once again, and the moment was suddenly up for grabs, since their targets had nowhere to run.

Block and Jocarto took the cue with all the lightning speed and precision of seasoned professionals, hauling out sound-suppressed Beretta 92-Fs, but Boshab's people split up, all snarls and curses, and rushed potential death as if they had this drill down from their own bad past encounters with treachery. Streams of converging 9 mm slugs from Block and Jocarto found the closest Pakistani, who was in the act of clearing his own weapon from hidden shoulder rigging. He almost made it, a Makarov pistol emerging, but only in time to crack out a round that punched a hole in plaster over the heads of the Z-Core kill team. The Pakistani's scream of outrage was cut short as he started dancing a mad jitterbug, trying to line up another shot even as crimson erupted from his chest in gory fountain spurts. A few more rounds tore into his chest, and he finally toppled to one side and brought down the dresser mirror in a rain of giant glass fangs.

And created just the sort of racket Jenkins had hoped to avoid.

Jenkins had his own worries, though, as one Pakistani flew in his face, spit gobs blowing from his vented mouth. A glimpse of another holstered weapon nearly clearing leather, and Jenkins pumped a 9 mm hollowpoint through the growling dark maw of his own charging beast. A chunk of the Pakistani's skull blew off as the slug cored out its exit, and he plummeted, hammering the floor with such force Jenkins imagined the walls were shaking by now. Somehow, a stroke of luck prevailed in the next moment, holding down the loud crash of the surviving Pakistanis.

Jenkins joined the old man and his own killers in chewing up the Pakistanis with enough rounds to ventilate them on both sides of their dancing bodies. The king-size bed cushioned their plunge before they slid to the floor.

When the old man pumped one round each into their heads for good measure, Jenkins found the specialist looked set to vomit. There were blood-spatter patterns over the bed, across the walls, but Jenkins found that only Timbers had been sprayed by all the flying blood. Stranger things had happened, he figured, and hoped their luck held.

The old man snapped the briefcase closed, snatched Timbers by the shoulder and yanked him out of his freeze. "Now, maybe you can see I am serious."

He addressed Block and Jocarto. "Follow us. Any pursuit shows, you are to initiate contact. And you will not fail."

The old man jacked the specialist toward the door, looked at Jenkins. "You have sixty seconds. Then we're gone."

Jenkins understood not only the need for haste and a rapid exit, but that he could get left behind to deal with the unpleasant chore of cleanup. He followed the old man out the door, then veered to the right. A quick search of the lot and the doorways on his march to the G-man. No curtains coming open even a few inches in the other rooms, no doorways disgorging the curious. No one in the office at that hour, either.

Smooth sailing. Jenkins was all alone, just his Beretta and the G-man. A few more steps down the lot, his focus like a laser beam on the face behind the windshield. The guy stiffened behind the wheel, and Jenkins lifted the Beretta.

THE ENEMY MADE its opening move, attempting to draw first and last blood, and lost. Thrust into some twilight zone of subversion and shadow assassins, where everyone but himself had something to hide, the Executioner was bent on taking this particular ride to the end.

Next stop, the motel off I-40 on the east edge of town. Bolan stuck to the posted speed limit as Rockwell reported his partner had just seen two men enter the room where the alleged Pakistani buyers of the Hellbox were waiting. Poe's intel package was woefully incomplete, and Bolan couldn't help but wonder if that was part of some insidious scheme. Why drop him in some dark borderland of intrigue, not even hand over the first name or even a face to run with, seek out, determine who was at the bottom of this alleged conspiracy? Hardly a clue to go on other than Poe's word the armed opposition was comprised of former soldiers and mercenaries, plus a smattering of ex-cons recruited out of prisons, here and overseas, as part of the backbone for this hard force called Z-Core.

From there on, though, the soldier would dig out the answers in the only way he knew how. By force, plain and simple.

The dull white oasis that passed for downtown Santa Rosa was little more than fading window dressing to Bolan as he alternated grim attention from the road ahead to the light traffic behind. No black unmarked vehicles turned up on his rear, at least not that he could see.

"If you're worried about the cops," Rockwell said, "forget about it."

Bolan glanced at Rockwell's expression of grim smugness. The Executioner had more than a few choice questions to put to the NSA agent but was going to let action speak volumes instead. Standard operating procedure whenever the soldier waded into a campaign, yes, but, in this instance, the truth would only get revealed if he torqued up the killing heat.

And instinct told him a bloodbath had only just begun.

The problem, though, of getting corralled by legitimate law enforcement was always a somber consideration for Bolan. Especially when the bodies started piling up in his wake, and on public property, no less.

"We just stepped into a war zone, Belasko of the Justice Department," Rockwell said, and Bolan wasn't certain for whose benefit he stated the obvious. "The cops are a nonfactor, the real ones that is. Groom Lake."

Bolan felt the tight pull on his lips as he bared his teeth a little. "What?"

"Area Fifty-One. It's the same setup here. We know how they interact with the local cops, the bottom line being they become the cops. What they've done in this and surrounding counties is insert their own people, at least on the county recorders, into the sheriff's department," he said, and shrugged. "Maybe even done the same on the city police force from here to Tucumcari, all the way back Albuquerque, highway patrol, too. Way it works, their suits are handed over badges and ID that state they are sworn and paid county sheriffs, deputized, the whole nine yards. They list a phony address or some P.O. box that doesn't exist on a zip code that doesn't exist, either. Try and break in on their radio frequencies sometime, and all you'll get are encrypted static bursts. My people did some cyber digging into the Federal Communications Commission, turned up zilch, then moved on through the Interdepartmental Radio Advisory Committee, which is the place where so-called legit government agencies get their alleged license for their own radio frequency. Turns out their frequency is registered to FEMA."

FEMA, again.

"Someone knew I was coming."

Bolan felt the freeze right away even as Rockwell kept his face blank.

"As in Mr. Poe."

"You tell me," Bolan said. "Was I expected?"

"I don't know, and that's the truth. Take it or leave it. If you think I'm setting you up to stick a blade in your back, you can drop me off now."

Bolan held the man's stare for a moment, once again grimly aware that only the persuasion of violence would strip off any mask of deceit, then faced the road.

"They were shooting at me, too, Belasko."

That much was true. Bolan glanced at the dings and white scars over the hood where Rockwell had come under fire. But...

The question of any treachery, Bolan suspected, whether it came from Rockwell or anyone else, would answer itself in due bloody course.

"We're almost there," Rockwell announced. "So, what's the plan?"

"The plan," the soldier mused, and spotted the pool of motels just off the interstate in the distance. "The plan is if I find a knife in my back, you can bet I'll find time enough to pull it out and return the gesture."

Rockwell seemed to think about that, then nodded and said, "Sounds fair enough."

And, for the moment, the Executioner let it go at that.

4

Bolan caught the angry edge but didn't quite hear the sincerity, even a note of desired vengeance behind the oath, to convince him Rockwell gave a damn one way or another about his slain comrade. Indeed, the soldier couldn't picture Rockwell sparing any time in the near future to mourn his dead partner.

That was assuming, of course, he ever cared at all, if Rockwell was even who and what he claimed to be. The longer he was in the man's presence, the more doubts Bolan had about Rockwell's motives, whatever they were to begin with. It wasn't something he could nail down, but the soldier considered himself better than a fair judge of character, and something definitely felt out of focus where Rockwell was concerned.

Bolan sensed the boundaries of the killing game rapidly closing in. His gut told him they were coming, shoot first, no one caring about the questions. It was simply a question of when and how many.

The corpse was slumped over the wheel, Bolan noting the windshield riddled with five bullet holes that fanned into a spiderweb. No point checking for a pulse, the end result was clear enough. From his viewpoint, just to the starboard front of the vehicle, the soldier could see half the guy's skull had been blown away where he sat. Bolan turned away, got his bearings and assimilated his next play.

No movement anywhere down the lot, motel doors sealed tight, curtains drawn. The guy might as well have met his violent fate in the middle of the Sahara. Well, if it worked for his killer, Bolan held fast to hope he could become just as invisible, skating on, no one the wiser. Basic fear or apathy on the part of civilians often worked to Bolan's advantage, but he never fully counted on the see-no-evil factor to clear him of a kill zone. The sky was brightening in golden bands, Mother Nature ready, he knew, to yield another day where travelers and tourists would soon be out in force in pursuit of breakfast or to pack up cars and kids for their next destination. Bolan counted ten vehicles, indicating far less than a capacity crowd, strung out in front of the doors. While they still slept, there was no better time, he figured, to unfurl his next course of action.

Much like a shark had to keep swimming to stay alive, a juggernaut had to keep rolling to maintain an impetus already gathered by initial but mounting aggression. To slow down meant to lose momentum. Losing momentum meant yielding ground, thus giving the enemy hope the tide could be turned, even rolled back to crush the oncoming blitz.

No mistake, Bolan was forging on, no slowing down, basic bulldoze, break and burn to the end of the line.

"Son of a bitch must have just walked up and started blasting," Rockwell said, sounding as if it were all just another day at the office. "Bosworth never knew what hit him."

"Another mess for that cleanup crew you mentioned?" Bolan asked.

Rockwell ignored the question, matched Bolan's sweeping surveillance of the office, the line of doorways, the lot. "No sign of that black SUV my partner mentioned with the two men who went in after the Pakistanis were inside."

"Which means they've bolted."

"But that's Major Boshab's Town Car," Rockwell said, and mentioned the room number where they were. Or had been. "What do you think it means?"

He could venture a guess but kept suspicions to himself, rearranging the game plan while basing his next move on a gamble the enemy was on the hunt, geared to come tearing in there, full-bore, content to leave another mess to the cleanup crew. He gave the engine some gas, rolled slowly away from the vehicle. The lot appeared large enough to accommodate any escape and evacuation in the SUV. First he needed to barge inside the targeted room, suspecting either some clue or yet more questions waited beyond the door. The idea—and Bolan had to admit to himself it wasn't one of his better ploys—was to make himself the bait, at least this time around. With any luck, if it went by the numbers the way he pictured it, he'd bag a prisoner. In Bolan's experience, though, luck was something he could create, and from there on he intended to make enough noise to win a cosmic lottery of blood victory.

He braked the SUV two doors down from where the Town Car was parked and where the Pakistanis were believed inside, in some form or other. But Bolan's hunch was the ISI major had been cut out of the loop. As Rockwell figured, his partner had been executed when the two men in question had left the room and vacated the premises. But why? Tying up some loose end? A simple but permanent blinding of watching eyes? Bolan checked his rear, put the vehicle in Park. He killed the engine, slipped the keys in his pants pocket. Unless four carloads of classified assassins roared up on the SUV, Bolan didn't foresee a problem driving off, even if that meant bulldozing his way to either side, racing out of the lot. Reaching over the seat, he unzipped the war bag, felt Rockwell watching him, itching to ask questions. One frag grenade disappeared into the pocket of his windbreaker, and he took the mini-Uzi, tucking the compact SMG inside the flap of his jacket

"I'm going in," Bolan told Rockwell, thrusting the door open. "Watch my back from the door. Some goons show up, give them a look, let them know you see them, then get inside the room."

"You planning on blowing up half the parking lot?" Rockwell asked, jerking a nod at the bulge in Bolan's pocket where the deadly egg rested.

"Do exactly what I say, and we may start to get some answers." The guy was giving him a funny look. "What? You said don't worry about cops showing up, right?"

"I've got your back, Belasko."

Bolan didn't care for the sound of that but kept the wry look off his face. In seconds flat, he made the door of the target room, Rockwell perching against the wall on the opposite side. The Executioner could sense the utter stillness of death beyond the door, a presence he'd come to know like a second skin over the years on his hell-fire sojourns. He let the silence hang for a moment, gave the surrounding environment another search and decided now was as good a time as ever.

He let the mini-Uzi drift out, muzzle leading the way, and opted to go in hard. A step back and the soldier aimed a stomp kick just below the doorknob. The door splintered where it met the jamb and the soldier charged inside, the mini-Uzi raking the murky interior. The coppery taint of spilled blood in his nose, he marched up to the slaughter. Four bodies, enough blood splattered around the room, he figured, to fill a tub. Fresh kills, skulls shattered and still leaking gore from the finishing touch. Their executioners had gone overboard, having damn near sheared the clothes off their chewed hides. The bodies were cooling but still warm to the touch as he knelt over the nearest corpse. Figure Rockwell's report from his fallen comrade, and the soldier guesstimated a twenty-minute jump, give or take, down the highway. Another look at the dead, even though Bolan didn't need to understand the overkill here to know the opposition was deadly serious.

"We've got company."

Rockwell was rolling inside, his expression neutral as he ran a quick look over the dead. "Black unmarked, no tags, just like the one at the diner. Two men. They spotted me, just like you wanted. Now what, Chief?"

Bolan stepped over the body stretched out in front of the dresser. Where he intended to take it all next, well, bloody footprints were the least of his concerns, assuming, of course, he made it out the door in one piece.

"Leave that door open. Get behind the far side of the bed and keep your head down."

FORCED TO WATCH the highway while nearly staring into the rising sun, Jenkins slipped on his dark sunglasses as he motored the SUV down the interstate.

"Take them both out. Yes, I know all about who he is. Sacrifices sometimes have to be made, you know this, and we've already lost three men. Your orders stand. I expect to hear back from you in two minutes sharp. Out."

Jenkins saw the old man meet his stare in the rearview mirror. Timbers was a quaking bundle of nerves in the back seat, looked as if he wished he could bail out the door, even if that meant bouncing off the asphalt at over sixty miles per hour and ending up a spewing sack of blood and broken bones. The specialist sat as far away from the old man as space would allow, Timbers seeming to Jenkins like a scolded child afraid of more punishment. It was understandable, given what little Jenkins knew about the guy's predicament. The specialist was in a world of shit, and what he did or didn't decide to do in the coming hours would seal the fate of his immediate family. And the old man would pump one round through his head, simply dump the body in a shallow grave in the desert. He'd done it before, hell, Jenkins had seen it himself.

But Timbers wasn't leaving the SUV on some flight out the door due to panic, a button on the driver's side panel having electronically locked all the doors. Still, the ex-merc felt contempt toward the specialist, glancing at his pink face in the rearview, entertaining a notion to personally shove the guy out, that little shit somehow commanding, it seemed, as much power and respect with his knowledge of the Hellbox as Jenkins would by the business end of his gun. Maybe life just sucked like that, he guessed, and couldn't help but wonder which was the more admirable profession between the two of them, if brains rather than brawn made a man more worthy in the eyes of the world. With that in mind, he decided there was something more unclean, even unholy about this whole spook business, the project called Opus Damocles. No defined agenda, trouble behind and maybe chasing them, his doubts and suspicions growing by the minute, the old man giving nothing up but wanting it all...

"Something you wish to ask, son?"

Jenkins let his gaze flicker off the old man's probing eyes as soon as he found Raven watching him. A look in the side glass to distract himself from his thoughts, and he spotted their rearguard maintaining roughly a quarter-mile distance. The latest strange one-way conversation he heard posed yet more questions. It sounded as if the old man personally knew one of the two shooters. That alone begged a whole slew of questions, but Jenkins decided to keep it simple.

"Yes, sir, there is."

"Well? Feel free to speak."

"Exactly what 'is' and 'about' to transpire here, sir?"

"You're referring to the Pakistanis?"

"Okay, for one thing, yes, sir."

"Expendables in the bigger picture. I was being truthful when I told them I had a better offer. And the plan has been altered somewhat, Mr. Jenkins."

"You people are insane," Timbers blurted, side-tracking Jenkins from his next question, which involved his role in that bigger picture. "You can't just run around, shooting men in cold blood. I'm a government employee, for God's sake, and you're telling me you intend to kidnap my family. For what? Money?"

"For your services. And God, Mr. Timbers, has nothing to do with this."

"What services?"

"I'll explain everything, Mr. Timbers, once we are safely at home base."

"Does that include me, too, sir?"

Jenkins watched something he couldn't pin down shadow through the old man's eyes as he looked out to the desert. "Just get us home, Mr. Jenkins, and I will explain everything to you, but I prefer to do it in more private surroundings."

Now what the hell did that mean? Jenkins wondered, and felt an invisible icy hand clutch at his bowels. At this point, with his own ass on the line, risking it all, executing men for reasons unknown, he figured the old man owed him some explanation, some clue to what the future held. A deep breath, and he managed to keep the anxiety and irritation off his face. In less than two minutes, he figured he would know something more. Or at least enough to determine how much of a threat their nameless pursuer from back east might pose. Whatever happened, Jenkins saw darkness ahead, even as the sun crept higher over the distant horizon.

BOLAN YANKED the pin but held the spoon on the frag grenade. Hunkered down on the far side of the dresser, the mini-Uzi poised to fire if his initial ploy went to hell, the Executioner caught the sound of two doors closing in the lot. Mentally he chalked off the distance, figured two doors down, close to his own vehicle, enemy approaching. Enough sunlight was cast from the east to hurl the shadows of the enemy over the lot beyond the door, silhouettes providing vague shapes of two men out there, but growing.

Closing.

The Executioner, though, didn't have to see them advancing to know they were nearly on the doorstep. He could feel them out there even as they rolled ahead, silent, faceless shapes, murder in their hearts.

Suddenly, he glimpsed Rockwell's image in one of two larger shards of glass that were supported by the dead Pakistani in front of the dresser. A quick look at Rockwell, and Bolan motioned with the hand clutching the grenade for the man to get down behind the bed and hold on.

The big bang was coming, and someone was seconds away from checking out. Bolan knew it was touch and go, no matter what, but he'd made the call to offer himself as human bait.

If they charged into the room, blazing away, the soldier would have to scrap his original idea. Only he was betting they'd take up positions on either side of the door—given the fact the enemy could plainly see evidence back down the road they were dealing with a determined warrior—and hit the interior with some spray and pray before some making some bulldog rush.

They did.

It looked like an Uzi submachine gun at first glimpse, as Bolan ducked back behind the dresser, the stammer of autofire splitting his senses, the wall reaching out from the bathroom behind his cover absorbing the first line of wild rounds in a drumming thud.

Factor the four-second time delay, and Bolan released the spoon.

One.

Plaster came showering over Bolan as the hornet's nest of steel-jacketed projectiles ripped into the walls and ceiling, side to side, another burst of autofire joining in to fuel the sound and fury and crank the racket up to new ear-shattering decibels.

Two.

And Bolan scrunched low, a lone strip of glass blasted off above his head by tracking autofire. He let the steel egg go, tossing it around the corner of the dresser, an underhand rolling pitch like some bowler releasing his ball down the lane, all but dammed up inside by adrenaline, anxious to see nothing but ten pins blasted and flying every which way.

Pressing himself against the wall, Bolan threw up an arm to shield his face from flying shrapnel, riding out the storm of lead chopping up the dresser, twin lines of searching bullets blowing past his cover a hail of glass, wood slivers and gristly strands of red flesh, taking hits and adding the ghoul's touch to deadly rain. Now, if only he timed the throw and the short distance right....

They were still shooting up the room when blast came. The soldier's world was rocked all to hell, the tight confines trapping the shock wave, hurling it back through the room on a boiling cloud of smoke, cleaving Bolan's brain with invisible spikes. The explosion hurtled countless steel bits, like flying piranhas, with the shrapnel eating the ceiling, the wall just ahead in a wave of barely audible thunks and chinks.

Beyond that, the soldier caught the brief scream of agony.

Strike.

The Executioner was rising, mini-Uzi up and searching the churning cloud ahead, when he found Rockwell mirrored and looming in the shard near his feet. The sudden deadly burn in the man's eyes, Bolan feeling that look bored into the side of his head, and the soldier made his move when the Glock lifted, only to vanish the next heartbeat into a void in the shard where there was no glass.

The Glock spit, but Rockwell was a microsecond and a fraction of an inch from scoring. The thought he was either lucky or blessed by cosmic intervention wanted to fleet through his mind, but Bolan was already dipping at the knees, anticipating the head shot, pivoting to return the gesture when hot lead scorched over his scalp. The mini-Uzi sweeping around, Bolan hit the trigger, riding the recoil as he drilled Rockwell in the gut, then sent another two, maybe three slugs coring into him just beneath the sternum. With the ringing from the grenade blast in his ears, it was hard to tell. Not that it made much difference in the end result, as Rockwell danced back, his legs pumping up and down in some bizarre aerobics number before he slammed into the wall, folded and slid for the carpet, leaving behind a dark smear on his plunge to the floor.

The soldier found he stood alone, nothing moving, not even a groan of misery beyond the fangs where the blast had remodeled the doorway.

"You dumb..."

Bolan saw the light fading fast in Rockwell's eyes. If the guy had left him any choice, Bolan would have taken him out at the knees. He needed answers more than he needed another kill. Some other avenue, then, beyond the door, out there in the desert.

Destiny.

The soldier angled himself, one eye on Rockwell, while monitoring the jagged maw with the mini-Uzi aimed across his body, just in case he'd only wounded one of the Classifieds.

"Why, Rockwell?"

"This...thing...it's bigger than any...one man...these people...they are shaping...the destiny...of...the world...."

Rockwell choked on his final words. Perhaps it was the simple heat of the killing moment, and Bolan had faced the Grim One more times than he could count, but there was something in Rockwell's eyes, even in death, that made him wonder what the hell this guy knew, what he'd really been all about. What secrets had this man taken to the grave?

Time to fly, and Bolan was moving into the swirl of cordite and drifting plaster dust when he discovered living in hope sometimes paid off.

The guy was croaking up his pain, eyes glazed, trying to focus on some distant point of craved relief, sliding along the walk on his belly like some serpent that had just been stepped on. A look to his left, and Bolan found nothing but a hunk of shredded beef, dully gleaming bone from the face, an arm and a leg staring him back where shrapnel had ground the body up, head to toe.

Point-blank, in the face. Quick, if nothing else.

One more step outside, and the soldier found the faces of fear poking out from doorways down the front of the motel. He saw the suit shimmy up on his hands and knees, some of the shock melting from his eyes. As luck, fear or speed would have it, the guy had cleared ground zero for the most part, maybe having caught sight of the grenade before it blew, sprinting a few yards from its lethal reach but not far enough.

Bolan had his prisoner. Grimly aware of the need for distance, he marched up to the croaker, grabbed what was left of his jacket and yanked him to his feet.

The Executioner jacked him toward the SUV. "Looks like this is your lucky day."

5

"I am a very important and respected individual in my field of specialty, which is, need I remind you, nuclear science. I am an invaluable asset to the United States military. I am even something of a celebrity in certain circles. You cannot do what you are doing to me. You will not hold my family ransom to force me to do whatever it is you intend. I have friends, men of power and means, high up. The Pentagon, FEMA, the Department of Energy. I know senators and congressmen. Someone will hear of this...criminal behavior. I am not some spook or some flunky with a weapon. I..."

When the backslap to the mouth came, sounding like a pistol shot from behind him, it was all Jenkins could do to keep the smile off his face. There, he thought, take that, Mr. Invaluable, and shut up.

"How dare you!"

"Would you like another?" the old man asked, gazing out the window, calm, in control.

Jenkins watched the specialist massage his mouth in

the rear glass, then dab at the line of blood running down his chin, finally staring with tears in his eyes at the red spot on his finger in mixed disbelief or horror. Timbers didn't look so special now.

"I didn't think so," the old man said.

The sideshow provided a moment of strange relief for Jenkins, and he suspected the old man had been looking to turn on some release valve for all the tension—strike that—"fear" the ex-merc had seen on his face the past twenty miles or so. Still more bad news, but oddly enough Jenkins found he wasn't surprised by the latest development. Part of the cleanup crew had been dispatched to the motel and reported back that, yes, there had been a clean sweep. Only it was the big shooter from back east who had done all the sweeping, sir. That was about as much as the old man offered to fill him in on. But it was crystal clear they were being dogged, perhaps even hunted by a professional. Whoever the nameless wonder from back east was, Jenkins knew he wasn't any government issue. It wasn't all that long ago, thirty minutes tops, but Jenkins could still vividly recall the flush that had turned the old man's face crimson, the high-tech cellular shaking in his hand for a full minute, the grim news apparently bringing on a sudden unnatural spell of Parkinson's. Some of the natural color was only now returning to the old man's complexion, but his head still had enough oscillating shake to it to warn Jenkins a human time bomb was sitting right behind him.

Jenkins had left the interstate several miles ago, now steering the SUV down one of the trails the Army Corps of Engineers had cleared for easy access by their vehicles to and from the compound. The network of trails connected them to the nearest outposts of civilization, but they also served as easy paths for recon of the desert. The old man had called in Blackbird One, apparently anxious to return to base. Even with the dirt strip clear of rocks and other debris, the ruts long since filled in by Army grunts laboring under the broiling sun, it was still another ninety-minute drive to the compound.

The old man touched base with the trailing team he'd ordered to fall behind. With the wireless earpiece in place, once again Jenkins was treated to a one-way conversation. Supposedly, the team was waiting in ambush for the mystery shooter's SUV. Or so went the plan.

The red mesa jutted out of the desert as Jenkins topped the rise, began a long descent for the chopper. Jenkins rolled ahead, braked just beyond the cyclone of dust whipped around by Blackbird One's rotor wash.

"Get out," the old man growled at Timbers, thrusting open his door but reaching over and dragging the specialist his way, either by accident or design banging some scalp off the edge before the scientist cleared his exit.

Stepping into the blazing sunlight, Jenkins was met by Mr. Trident, ex-Marine Recon and former guest on the State of Florida's Death Row for murdering his wife. Jenkins returned the salute while Trident, an HK MP-5 subgun hung around his shoulder, swept past and took the SUV's wheel.

"Now, Mr. Timbers," the old man said, shoving the specialist away. "Here it is. One call, I can exterminate not only your immediate family, but I have the power and the authority to wipe out your entire bloodline. What you, sir, fail to understand is that I *am* the law. The fact of the matter is, sir, I am so powerful, I can reach into the very futures of your children's children and render them sterile with a little something extra the next time they pour themselves a glass of tap water. When I order you to do something you will do it."

"My mind is made up. I'm calling your bluff."

The old man seemed to think about something, Jenkins braced for the pistol to come out and put one between the geek's eyes. It never happened. Instead, the old man nodded. "Very well. The highway isn't that far back. Let's go, Mr. Jenkins."

Timbers shot a look toward the SUV as it motored through the dust storm to pick up the long run down the trail. "What? In this heat. No water. You're going to leave me stranded here?"

"You're free to go."

Timbers sputtered something about consequences and repercussions, but Jenkins was already in lockstep with the old man, forging into the rotor wash, hopping into Blackbird One's belly. The old man veered off to the cockpit and told the pilot, "You know what to do."

Jenkins settled on a cushioned bench as the pilot closed the door to the fuselage by electronic touch. Curious, Jenkins saw the old man reach inside a shelf beneath a camera monitor mounted on the wall just to the right of the cockpit doorway. He inserted a video cassette into the VCR, used the small remote to power up both machines, the figure of Timbers flashing in living color up there on the monitor. Jenkins felt the chopper rise, easing ahead, then hovering close to Timbers, who was stumbling along in something of an angry daze. Timbers was shielding his face, mouthing something into the camera, when the sky opened up on the specialist, raining blood and thunder. The first few 7.62 mm rounds knocked Timbers off his feet, his head exploding next, all but obliterated, with a crimson-gray halo holding above the shoulders a moment before the real gore took to the air.

"That's the penalty for even mere insubordination," Jenkins heard the old man say, and wondered if he was meant to read between the lines. "Ah, well. We still have the others. Should they need a little convincing, there will be film at six. That would be chow time."

The double pounding of miniguns kept up for the better part of another half minute. By the time they were finished, Jenkins saw there wasn't enough of Timbers left to feed a buzzard.

"He doesn't look so important now, does he, Mr. Jenkins?"

"WHAT'S YOUR NAME?"

"Freeman."

"What were you before this Z-Core?"

The long face, with its lantern jaw, turned and gave Bolan a look of fleeting surprise. "Ex-Beret. Saw some action during the Gulf War. Came back, found I was sick all the time, could hardly get out of bed unless I was juiced on dope. Started with prescription stuff, then moved on to my own sources. Whacked out one night, broke, generally pissed at Uncle Sam and the world, I got collared after I hit a pharmacy. Shot the place up, or so they said, since to this day I can't remember too clear the events that transpired. Me and my trusty M-16, ex-Gulf War hero turned junkie. No one bothered to tell me, or so I heard through the void, how the Iraqis were using chemical and maybe biological weapons. Mined Kuwait and parts of Iraq when they bailed back for the comfort of Saddam's bosom. Must have touched off the mines on their retreat, released their silent killers. Guess it was just my tough luck I operated behind enemy lines long enough to catch a few deep whiffs of whatever the shit was."

"You picked the wrong team this time around."

"Tell me about it."

Bolan had cleared the limits of Santa Rosa, rolling east into the harsh blaze where the sun was already baking the desert into a shimmering furnace. He watched the highway, front and back, from behind dark aviator shades. He'd already frisked Freeman and found him clean. The ex-Green Beret was in bad shape, bleeding all over the seat from any number of wounds where flying shrapnel had eaten up his hide, the back of his skull a mottled patchwork of cuts and gashes, running and dried blood. Not mortal wounds, perhaps, but Bolan knew the man could use some medical attention. Right then the Executioner had far more weighty concerns than Freeman's pain and discomfort. No black unmarked vehicles minus license plates had turned up yet, but Bolan knew the authority behind the suits was most likely staging another round of mayhem meant to check him out. In broad daylight, the odds weren't in Bolan's favor if he found himself locked in some protracted desert war. He worked best under the cover of night, using the shadows to stalk human prey as if the darkness itself was a tool in his proved skilled and lethal hands.

The soldier would take the chips were they fell. His mind was made up, though, in the respect that he was going for their compound. A soft probe, at least that was the plan, see what was what, then make a judgment call.

"Man, I hurt. But I guess I'm looking at the wrong guy for a dose of sympathy."

"They say you can find that in the dictionary."

"Yeah, between shit and syphilis."

"It could be worse."

"Right, I told my partner how he ought to consider not drinking whiskey on the job. Jimbo never saw it coming."

"His troubles are over."

"Uh-huh. Meaning mine have just begun."

"Depends on you."

Bolan pulled out the swipe card, held it up for Freeman to have a look.

"You can swipe it to get out, but you'll need the access code off the guy you took it from to get in. I understand he's unavailable."

"How about yours?"

He handed it over, no sweat, chuckling, and rattled off a series of numbers. "So, you're just going to walk right in there, have a look around, write up a field report how things are a little hinky out here in New Mexico."

"Maybe, minus the field report. Or maybe there's another option. Show me the quickest way to get there."

"About five, six miles up ahead, I think. There's a track been smoothed out. Leads right to it."

Bolan reached behind the seat, took the state map

and put it in Freeman's hands. He watched the former Green Beret trace the track with his finger, stab the spot where the compound was planted. Barring further attempts on his life, and Bolan anticipated the enemy turning up the heat, he figured he could reach the area sometime just after noon.

"How many shooters in your Z-Core?"

"Man, this is rich. I'm riding with the Terminator himself. Okay, big guy, thirty. They rotate us out every three months. Bring in a fresh crew. You know, I was one day from getting a stretch of R and R. Looks like that beach and a piña colada will have to wait, huh?"

"I'll be interrupting a lot of vacations soon enough."

"You'll never get close. They've got more surveillance, security, infrared, heat-seeking, black helicopters with enough firepower to take out a place the size of Santa Rosa. Man, they've got these little robots, space-age stuff, look like big scorpions, creeping around the desert, beaming back so much as a rattler in the shade."

"Mines? Booby traps?"

"No. Guess they don't want some nature lover blowing his leg off and raising enough racket to bring a horde of reporters out here to have a closer look."

"And the way down this track?"

"Same thing. Watching eyes. They'll know you're coming."

So be it. Despite Freeman's celluloid comparison, Bolan was flesh and blood, and it was never part of the plan to simply wade into the guns, a gung-ho charge, risking it all in some bulldoze play. Sometimes, though, the soldier had to issue the challenge, bring the enemy to him, lined up in his gun sights. In this instance, the hunter could just as easily become the hunted, and waiting for an armed problem to head his way wasn't a working option, not if he intended to walk out the other side. Sometimes there was little choice other than a grim, determined march right down the opposition's gullet. Five down so far, six, including his passenger, but he was still facing long odds. So, what was new?

"What's their angle, as far as this Hellbox goes?"

"Angle?"

"They're selling it," Bolan stated, and was treated to a look that told him Freeman was wondering where he came by his information.

"I caught some scuttlebutt. They've got three of them right now, down there in the bowels of the place, packed up and ready to be shipped out."

"Where and when?"

"I couldn't tell you. Way I saw it, they've got two semis, figure they're going to be trucked out. The old man, I hear, is getting antsy."

"The old man?"

"Yeah, he's in charge. He's what they call in spook speak a floater. No clue what agency he pledges allegiance to. All I know is that he's who we take our orders from, him or Jenkins, an ex-mercenary who did two stretches in prisons in Angola and Pakistan."

"And they just opened the gates and let him walk off into the sunset?"

"Just like me. Only in my case, there was a signed

order from the judge who sentenced me to a flat decade. Lawyer comes in one day, something about the witnesses gave false testimony, the cops supposedly catching the real bad guy. Walked out of Angola, and the old man was there waiting for me in a stretch limo. Handed over a blank check but told me no more than three zeroes."

"I don't hear any accent."

"I was born in Indiana."

"Give me the layout of this complex."

Bolan listened as Freeman filled him. The soldier was looking north, thinking the complex didn't sound too elaborate other than its high-tech surveillance net, when he spotted the spool of dust, made out the dark shape of the SUV. A check of the mileage, and Bolan figured they were coming up to the track. He watched the SUV bouncing over the rough terrain, bearing a hard course slightly northeast. A minute later it jounced up an incline, dipped over the edge and was gone from sight where the scrubland was broken up by a series of humps that passed for hills. Searching the highway and the sweeping desert to both sides, Bolan couldn't find any pursuit other than the solitary SUV. That didn't mean, of course, there weren't other vehicles on the roll even then to cut him off as soon as he made the track. And it would take all of two seconds from a sudden visit by a black helicopter to spread him all over the desert.

"There."

Bolan glanced in the side glass at a Honda Civic in his wake, gently put on the brakes as he spotted the mouth of the track Freeman was pointing to.

"Man, I'm thirsty. You got any water in here?"

There was a canteen in his war bag, and the soldier decided to make a brief stop, suspecting he needed to add a little more walking-around firepower. The Executioner reckoned that desert war was about to come to him, after all.

6

Range was just under four hundred meters, no wind to speak of, the mental adjustment for a slight downward trajectory to target calculated. Getting the focus on the Hensoldt ZF 10x42 telescopic sight homed in on the bastard's SUV as it swung off the highway and rolled down the embankment, it should be no fuss, no muss to drill them both.

Good to go.

But the operative word, Mark Longley thought, was *should*. Whoever the big guy in black was he had proved himself no green slouch when it came to kicking ass and taking names. The way Longley had heard it from the old man, the bastard had cut down five of their own so far like they were...what? Nothing? Cherries, fresh out of officer candidate school, wide-eyed and bushy-tailed, naive as hell about the real price of locking horns with the other guy on the battlefield?

For a moment it boggled his mind. Those dead men he had known and worked with—battle-scarred pros with plenty of blood on their hands—had bitten the dust before they seemed to know what hit them, the shooter mowing them down as easy as swatting flies. Unbelievable, the whole outrage demanding payback, if nothing else. Some government law-enforcement agency or intelligence outfit had cut their man loose to come out here and queer the project. That by itself begged a list of questions, a whole load of problems now engineered and on the drawing board, thrown in their faces by the simple fact some mystery shooter had a hunch all was not what it seemed in New Mexico. But all the answers up to then had come blasting out of the bastard's guns. One bullet for each problem that flew his way.

Screw the guy.

It was time to put a stop to the nonsense, and he considered himself just the right man for the job. After all, he hadn't earned his medals—number-one marksman, just for starters—during his stint in the Army's Special Forces because he was a dreamer from the Bronx who sat on the sidelines, indulging fantasy tripe, while the other guys grabbed the brass ring. No, sir, even beyond the Army—bumping into Jenkins in a waterfront bar in Marseilles, as some fluke of fate had it, if he cared to recall that first encounter—and he had long since proved to himself and a few dozen corpses piled over there in Angola and Mozambique he was a soldier with the talent and the balls to make dreams reality.

The difference between now and then was this guy wasn't some unsuspecting UNITA or FRELIMO amateur he'd dropped with a rifle from eight to a thousand meters out while Jenkins and a pack of war dogs raided some lonely outpost in the bush. To some degree, though, in hindsight, the mercenary days were cleaner in motive and circumstance, where personal freedom was won or lost by how much blood they shed, who they greased along the way to steer them clear of some African backwater. The paychecks from their South African "businessmen" weren't as hefty as the blank check he received when he was rotated out every few months from the compound, but the risk he could end up before some Congress weasels, soft pink faces whining at him about military conspiracies and demanding for the people they allegedly served to know what the hell his involvement...well, the prospect of riding out a long stretch in Leavenworth was as real as the .308 Winchester Magnum rounds he was ready to drive through flesh and blood. The gig was all spook stuff, handled by shadow men with their own agenda, blank checks and doublespeak where he couldn't get a straight answer from up top unless someone took a chain saw and threatened to cleave off an arm or leg. And even then...

Again, he didn't see the problem in his skill to deliver the killshots. And the Heckler & Koch MSG-90 A-1 was a brand-spanking-new state-of-the art sniper's wet dream come true, damn near, he figured, off the assembly line. Nearly three pounds of this updated version of the PSG-1 had been trimmed off, and he knew he could go on forever about permanent-welded sight-mount pedestals, the entire sight mounting system...

It was more than enough, he decided, to get the job done, and right the first time around.

And he was ready to unload. Computer-enhanced sat visuals, and the lay of the land was always pored over back at base, the guys at the top figuring the troops would need to know every nook, cranny and gulley beyond the compound in the event the just such a moment like this arose and the terrain could become their ally.

He lifted from his prone position, peering over the lip of the gulley, settled on a knee. Jackson was making the run for the planned intercept. The idea, at least in concept, was for the bastard to balk when he found the track blocked by their wheels, Jackson holding his ground with an Uzi aimed the guy's direction. If the guy slowed down, Longley could serve up some easy buzzard meat. He had only two problems with the whole setup. One, the sun was beating his way from the east, but he figured his point of concealment coupled with distance would shield him well enough if the bastard cared to give the scrubland anything more than a sweeping eye. The other problem was the old man's order to kill one of their own. After he and Jackson had spotted the SUV blow past their hiding roost off the road, they'd called the old man back. It had pretty much been a blur, but they saw enough to know the nameless shooter had bagged Freeman. Capture, especially by someone who may or may not be linked to a legitimate government agency, wasn't an option. If Freeman had been persuaded to start singing the blues to buy a little peace of mind for himself at the expense of the project...

It wouldn't matter.

The nylon satchel beside him had clips to spare if, by some fluke, he missed the first shot out of the gate. Three 5- and three 2-round detachable box magazines, two of the 50-round drum kind if the SUV attempted some rabbit run up the track were within easy reach. A part of him hoped the bastard made a run for it. It would give him a chance to familiarize himself a little more with the rifle, fine-tune skills that had for too long been shelved.

Longley watched as the SUV hit the track. The bastard was on his clock now, and Longley felt the slow burn of adrenaline as he lifted the sniper rifle. Jackson braked, north, a few hundred yards or so ahead, then stopped, waiting for the show to begin. Their plan looked set to unfold like some magic carpet begging the fulfillment of their hopes and dreams when the mark actually slowed up, then brought the SUV to a full halt in a cloud of trailing dust.

What happened next brought a smile to Longley's face. Both men stepped out of the vehicle, but on the passenger side. Had his prime target spotted him?

Whatever, in the final analysis it didn't matter. He was pumped to shoot two rats in a barrel. For a ghosting second, he believed it was almost too good to be true, and he knew what they said about that. Even still, he decided if the bastard was going to make it this easy why not indulge the guy's death wish?

THE SOLDIER KNEW there was no point in a casual move to beef up the hardware. Even if he wanted to give it the appearance of a pit stop, either for a water break or subtle read of his surroundings, they were there and waiting to drop the hammer. That much was certain, but where did the soldier take it from there? Something didn't feel right to Bolan about the whole encounter, some ploy on their part that should have been obvious. But what? The SUV was just off the track, perched up there a few hundred yards away, more or less. Engine running. A tall black man stepped out, a couple easy strides settling him at a point on the far side of his vehicle. The human roadblock lifted an Uzi submachine into Bolan's view.

So where were the others?

Bolan hauled out two frag grenades, dumped them in a pocket of his windbreaker. Whatever was about to happen he was ready to pick up the pace, throw it back. The mini-Uzi went around his shoulder, the warrior taking the M-16, chambering a round before he stuffed the M-203's breech with a 40 mm grenade.

All set. Or was he? And primed for what?

The direction from where the opposition's vehicle came gave him pause to think it through. Sliding out the door on Freeman's side was logical enough, since his hunch was one or more gunners had been dropped off somewhere to the east, hunched somewhere, poised and itching for an easy shot. And the wheelman's stand indicated an intended barricade or intercept point. Or was he waiting on the cavalry? A check behind on the highway, and Bolan watched a few vehicles fly past in both directions.

Bolan had already handed off the canteen. He was watching Freeman gulping down the water, his bloodied passenger leaning against the fender, when it happened.

It was a flash, winking for the briefest moment against the sun, but it was more than ample evidence for Bolan to know the sniper had gone to work.

"Get down!" Bolan told Freeman, the soldier dropping low behind the passenger door. He thought he heard the shot, echoing over the broken tableland, but with the sudden burst of adrenaline and the pounding of his heartbeat in his ears he couldn't be sure. Freeman was caught looking up the track toward his comrade, as if questioning the moment, then swiveling a puzzled expression Bolan's way, when the bullet slammed into the back of his head. The face of confusion was obliterated, the slug tunneling an exit out Freeman's forehead on a crimson blast just above the nose. No sound next, except the crunch of deadweight on unyielding earth.

The Executioner threw himself ahead like a low-flying missile, cracked open the door and slid in a furious crabbing surge over the passenger's seat. He left the M-16, stock facing up, canted from the vacated cushion but pointed his way for a quick grab. Decision made to ram it up the enemy's gut, and Bolan dropped the SUV into Drive. He hunched his bulk as best he could against the door panel, inches below the window, while squeezing his legs under the steering wheel.

Aware just enough of his head might be framed in crosshairs, lending the sniper another view to end it, Bolan lowered himself on instinct an eyeblink before the glass above blew in over his head, slivers flaying over his scalp like angry bee stings. He stamped the gas pedal, lurched up and took the wheel, cutting a short zigzag back and forth across the track, grim hope the wild turns would throw the sniper's sights off him long enough for the soldier to launch a flying bulldoze counterattack. Bolan floored it, tapped the brakes, jerked around in his seat, then laid on the gas again. He shot the needle up just past forty, lining up the metallic rhino charge on the SUV ahead. He had the distance to impact shaved by nearly half, keeping himself as low beneath the wheel as possible, when Mr. Barricade ripped loose with the Uzi. The windshield caved to the 9 mm onslaught, the soldier closing his eyelids to slits as the flying blanket of glass tumbled in chunks and needles over his head. Tracking autofire skidded off the hood in a thudding barrage that shimmied the steering wheel in his grip but told Bolan the shooter ahead was holding his ground, pouring it on.

And Bolan clung to deadly hope he could pull it off. The storm ended, and Bolan could visualize the guy's face of fear, Mr. Barricade figuring out his intention before he either bolted for the wheel or fell back to clear the coming crash.

A quick look over the steering wheel, the nose of his SUV zeroed in and roaring on for impact, holding true to the mental map he'd pictured, and Bolan glimpsed the guy flapping his arms, shock on his face as bright from the soldier's adrenalized perspective as the blazing sunshine.

The guy might have made it if he had been more inclined to flight instead of fight.

The Executioner crushed on the brakes, braced for collision. The hardman backpedaled, stumbled, fear carving his face and holding in the Executioner's sight like a deer frozen in the headlights. The tail end of Bolan's rocket ride was skidding, tires digging at dirt, when he drilled the SUV.

LONGLEY WAS STUNNED at first, then annoyed with himself that he'd missed his chance to nail the bastard. But what could he do? The guy had ducked, just like that, there then gone. And who the hell was this guy? One second Longley had him sighted in, larger than life in living color in his crosshairs, ready to take his head off at the shoulders, then the guy swung his way, damn near staring into the scope before he hit the deck, almost as if the mystery man had some built-in radar, a mental blipping aiming straight from him to the sniper's nest.

Almost psychic, he reconsidered, and didn't care much for the raw, dry oven of his mouth, a nagging fear holding him immobile for a long moment.

No, scratch that ESP bull, he thought, and cursed. Mirrored sun flash had robbed him of the glory, and now it all looked in serious doubt he'd get another opportunity to haul his bloody trophy back to the compound and put that subtle inquiry to the old man about a bonus. What the hell, huh? Figuring one out of two would have done for the time being, the impulse had been to turn the rifle on Freeman and take care of that problem. If little else—and it was damn little for his money—a potential squawker was shut up for good.

All that seemed like an hour ago now. The human bull was charging. Longley watched Jackson get cut out of the picture next, his buddy sent reeling to his ass as the ground behind seemed to open up, only it was some break in the terrain where a flash flood had carved up the stretch to his comrade's rear, claimed his fall. Feeling some morbid dread crossed with grim admiration, Longley found himself torn between lining up another shot and spectating.

Their SUV was rammed, jumped up on its port wheels on impact, seemed to hang in the dust cloud blowing over it before it dropped back in place. All that dust, Longley licking the sweat on his lips, and where was the bastard? Before he made a clear visual, the bastard was out of his vehicle, an assault rifle flaming away, the big guy charging ahead, low around the SUV's front end.

Jackson was chopped up, left where he fell to twitch and bleed out.

Longley weighed two options. He lost sight of the

nameless wonder even as he saw the door behind the driver's side crack open. Wait a second! If the guy was digging through the big nylon bag, claiming spoils of war...

Okay, slow down, assess his next move. Did he start shooting up the vehicles down there, force it into some game of man-to-man stalk on foot? he wondered. No. That would leave him stranded. A long trudge back to the compound, in heat known to suck the life out of a man in a couple hours flat, no choice even for a tough nut like himself. He was on his own, one hundred percent, since he flung number-two option out the window almost as soon as it danced into his thoughts. Calling back to the old man for help was definitely not the way to earn an extra blank check. Not to mention it would sound like he couldn't handle it on his own, talent and balls in question, maybe the old man even smelling some cowardice on his end.

No cavalry then.

Just one sniper, the best around, in his mind, his rifle and some crazy bastard who'd gotten lucky to get this far.

Out loud, Longley urged the nameless wonder to get in gear and come charging his way.

BOLAN'S DECISION was absolute and concrete, even though there really was no choice. He'd already kicked open the door with his bull charge, called the action and invited the do-or-die stand. Leaving any threat stalking his rear while he rolled on for the compound was a recipe for disaster. The Executioner had dialed the heat up way past blistering anyway, and he was charging on. Why slow down now, simply let them lick their wounds, regroup? One sniper, anyway, was positioned about four hundred feet to the west. The Executioner mapped out a mental course of action, an encore variation of his bulldoze tactic that had ended with a quick M-16 burst to the hardman's chest.

The enemy's war bag was an added bonus, saving the soldier the problem of burning up his own supply of ammo on one sniper. Sticking close to the floorboards, scrunched in the space between the driver's seat and the back seat, he peeked inside the bag. And found grenades to add to his arsenal, enough extra clips for an Uzi subgun that the guy he'd just waxed wouldn't need anymore. Beside the Benelli M-1014 12-gauge semiautomatic shotgun and boxes of shells, he saw two thermal imaging cameras, a portable laptop, probably with an LCD panel, a working viewfinder that could be hooked to the infrared devices. The high-tech radiation liberators might come in handy if there was night hunting to be done. Assuming he even got as far as the compound.

Digging deeper, he hit the jackpot.

The Executioner filled his hand with an HK 69 grenade launcher, fished around and came up with a pouch stuffed with 40 mm missiles, about a dozen altogether. The soldier moved quickly, feeling the sniper out there, the enemy searching for any opening to start blasting, Bolan's combat senses fired up, tuned in to the shooter's presence like a moth might be drawn to the flame. He filled the handheld launcher with a cylindrical 40 mm charge, knew the weapon could also be fitted to all HK assault rifles—if the need arose—backed out, shut the door, then moved ahead and went in low to take the wheel.

The back window erupted, detonated glass flying for Bolan, pinging off the interior as he put the SUV into Drive, hit the wheel to the right and whiplashed around his commandeered bulldozer. Two full tight circles, weaving a brown wall around the SUV, throwing up a temporary shroud while hoping to give the sniper some more anxiety to chew on, and Bolan knew it was now or never. Pedal stomped, he raced out of the dust storm, the front end lurching as the wheels slammed off a rut. The mad gyration threw the sniper's aim off the mark, Bolan flinching instinctively as the hole appeared in the windshield without a sound, a foot from his face, his eyelids slitted against the spray of chips. Bolan cut the wheel side to side, dropping low enough to keep the shooter from getting a clear fix while he marked off the spot where the sniper was perched, spied him clinging to his piece of barren turf up the low rise.

Shaving the gap in two, he leveled out the SUV, aimed its nose for an arrow-straight course where the sniper seemed hell-bent to fight it out where he stood. Easing off the gas, Bolan let it coast another fifty yards or so, the speed dropping to roughly twenty miles an hour, a bullet screaming off the hood to starboard. Nothing more than a glance at the earth beyond his door, but it was enough to spy some tumbleweed coming into view.

The windshield was lost in a giant tumble of shards as Bolan opened the door and bailed, timing his flight and anticipated drop to the tumbleweed. Hands filled with the M-16 and the stubby grenade launcher, Bolan braced for a hard touchdown. The tumbleweed cushioned his landing, as he hoped, the soldier allowing momentum to carry him into a roll, grunting as he felt the grenades in his pocket digging into his side. He came out of the roll, leaped to his feet, sprinting for the rear of the SUV. It was rolling up the rocky grade, the sniper darting to the side, trying like hell to line up one last shot. Bolan triggered the launcher on the fly, a hasty shot, not meant to score a kill, but rather distract the shooter long enough to give the soldier another try on the run. The thunderclap erupted closer to the sniper than Bolan had counted on, the soldier offering brief silent thanks to Lady Luck. The SUV was losing steam as it climbed the rise, Bolan falling in behind the vehicle, opting for the M-16 to finish it as the sniper sailed away from the boiling cloud. The enemy gunner managed to hold on to his rifle, either determined or maybe desperate enough to cling to some fading hope he could still break the soldier's banzai charge.

Whatever hope lit the eyes and cleared away the dazed and confused expression above Bolan lasted all of two seconds. The Executioner shot from the hip, on the run, the swarm of 5.56 mm projectiles carving the sniper from crotch to sternum. A few more rounds stuttering from the assault rifle, and Bolan dropped the sniper on his back, limbs twitching out the life before wilting into limp rubber.

Another unexpected gift from his enemies waiting for him when he reached the corpse. The Executioner felt the adrenaline peter off, a fizzling spark in his blood as he scoured the land stretching away, turning in all directions.

Traffic was picking up, a few more vehicles sweeping down the highway with the advent of full-blown morning. Distance enough to the kill zone would keep them wondering if some mirage was fooling with their eyes, or maybe travelers were just clearing the cobwebs of sleep, focused on the road ahead, Bolan couldn't be sure. No one out there slowed down or appeared they could be bothered with an exploration of a violent unknown.

The soldier claimed the sniper's rifle and the bag of clips and drums. He watched the SUV bounce and shudder over the broken ground, losing momentum where the ground stretched away in a flat tabletop from the sniper's former lair. A few more minutes, retrieving his own wheels, then a short run to gather in the spoils these two had given up, and the soldier intended to keep an appointment with destiny.

He checked the skies for a black helicopter but found he was clear and free of any flying threat for the moment. Nothing at all he could see above and out there to betray a human predator, at least.

And Bolan looked away from the dark shape of a lone buzzard riding the heat thermals, waiting on breakfast.

7

Standing there, watching the craggy moonscape fanning away from the compound to touch the distant horizon, sweating under a broiling early-afternoon sun, so hot, in fact, it could have been the eye of the devil glaring down with malicious intent, Jenkins felt like the loneliest SOB on earth.

So, what was new? A haunting weight suddenly fell on his shoulders, and he wondered why in the world he would pick a time like this to kick around the yesterdays that had made him the man he was today. Roll with it, why not, he told himself.

Hell, he'd always been on his own, anyway, some design by a cruel fate, he figured, forced over the years by a cosmic touch to prove his worth and mettle among men more times than he could count. Eventually, God willing, he would hold up to display a pair of Godzilla-size stones after the killing ended, showing the doubters and the cynics he had the right stuff. That he could, in fact, sit among their sacred ranks, one of the troops, basking in the booze-soaked glory of battles won, enemies slain, all that remembrance that never meant jack shit when the next round of bullets started flying.

It never panned out that way, at least in their eyes. He was a soldier of fortune in the end, killing for a buck, protecting and advancing the vested interests of men in thousand-dollar suits who thought they had the world by the short hairs. So then, why bother?

He wasn't one of them, never would be, and strangely enough, that gave him some range of comfort, and a new bout of energized pride swelled his limbs. Why, though, plague his thoughts with bitter recall?

The old man, that was why, the smug know-it-all...

Worlds apart. So be it.

Prison life had been no day at the beach, either. Try telling that, though, to some medalled vet—sloshed and reduced by selective memory and vats of bourbon to walking goo, blubbering on about this and that battle and such—that he had done his time like a man, lived through another kind of war altogether. He'd killed, bare hands, some knife-wielding thug over there, where he'd been dumped into a hellhole that would have made the Marquis de Sade's dungeon digs look like a penthouse suite at the Hilton. What the hell did they know, anyway? Try walking a hundred paces in his shoes. If they could. He was a soldier, dammit, tried and proved.

For some reason, though, the past wanted him to kick the present square in the ass, in fact, have him rage like a demon, force some issues hanging, and from the business end of his subgun. Suddenly, his mysterious mentor and benefactor struck him like those old-timers hashing over past glory, some light in the old man's eyes, burning with yesterday's recall of victory but still in search of some blinding ray of future greatness.

Like he could get it, just reach out and take what he wanted, the eyes telling the world at large he couldn't, no, *wouldn't* be denied.

The world was his personal chess game.

He shoved those thoughts from his mind. Duty beckoned, even if he didn't like it.

Armed with the latest batch of orders while receiving yet another grumbled monosyllabic burst from the old man—no contact with the last team, the running assumption now that Jackson and Longley were dead meat left behind for the buzzards—and still more fuel was tossed on the fire of the grave reservations Jenkins had about the immediate future.

Getting worse all the time, the more he thought about the situation.

The forklifts were trundling out the crates, a rolling assembly line of man and machine loading up the two black eighteen-wheelers, hauling out the cargo from the bowels of the compound, when Saunders stepped forth. Jenkins read the doubt on the face of the former Army sergeant-turned-bank-robber-murderer. Jenkins had coined a term for those men under his command who had been snatched, thanks to subversive or outright threatening manipulation of the legal system, from the clutches of the Grim Reaper.

Death Row Soldiers.

He kept that title to himself, never using the term out

loud, some superstitious impulse always keeping his tongue at bay whenever he felt inclined to announce what he thought of as a clever little tag. As if it was something to be proud of on their part, cheating death, granted new life when all hope looked lost.

Somehow, aware Saunders's eyes echoed the same questions that rooted Jenkins to parched brown dirt, the ominous catch title was no longer a tainted badge of honor in his mind. Death was out there, and it was coming. Incredibly enough, one man was threatening to bring down the roof, dismantle the project, scrap the hopes and dreams of the powers up top. Which made Jenkins wonder what the hell the old man was thinking with the new round of orders. Was the old man losing it, some senile childish fervor goading him on to meet this badass in the flesh? And do what if the badass was brought to him in one piece? Recruit the bastard? Offer the guy a blank check? It didn't make sense, and Jenkins was sure Saunders wanted to point that out.

"Permission to speak, sir?"

Jenkins ran a look up and down the brown hill. He knew there were cameras, minirobots clanking around, heat-seeking and infrared surveillance devices not even his own trained eye could detect. Maybe even a listening device or two, some miniparabolic mike buried in a crack hardly wide enough to accommodate a wandering scorpion. Maybe the old man was even right then watching, ears tuned in, on the edge of his seat, paranoia further inflamed by a glass of whiskey. Screw it.

"Granted."

"Are you sure you heard him right, sir? We are to capture this individual? Shoot only to wound, if forced to? This guy, whoever he is, has capped, what? Six, seven of our men already?"

"Those are the orders, Mr. Saunders. If you have a problem with them, I suggest you talk to the boss."

And that ended any further discussion.

Jenkins looked to his two three-man units. Grouped near the two black choppers, they were checking gear, weapons, ready to move out. They were all armed with their HK MP-5 subguns, but Jenkins knew they were more beasts of burden at the moment than tools of death. Six soldiers then, a few of them scowling and glaring over the toys they would carry to predetermined points of ambush. There were pepper spray handguns, rifles that could shoot electric charges or spew out steel nets. Handheld Tasers, pistols that would fire hypodermics full of tranquilizer. Gas masks attached to webbing in the event one of them tossed a tear gas canister. They struck Jenkins more like a convention of Star Trek groupies than battle-tried soldiers.

Whatever. Orders were orders. If it went to hell again, at least he could wash his hands of any coming bloody fiasco.

His radio crackled with the old man's voice. "Mr. Jenkins."

"Fall out," Jenkins ordered Saunders by way of dismissal, and wondered if the old man had spied their encounter.

"Jenkins here, sir."

"We are assembled. Report here immediately."

"Yes, sir, I'm on the way."

They were waiting for him in what the old man simply called the Room. Jenkins was clueless as to the identity of the four men who had choppered to the compound, but one of them was festooned with enough brass to warn him the stakes here were going up. Something was in the wings, and he suspected the project was shifting to some other dimension, deeper into a borderland of shadows and yet more Chinese boxes, everything that was before now in motion about to be accelerated. To what conclusion? Where did it all go from here? What was the critical mass of their goal?

He turned away as his hunting expedition headed out, wondered next if he was indulging wishful thinking, hoping that someone soon would shed light on dark questions that kept building in his mind.

He couldn't be sure, not yet, but something warned Jenkins he was about to face the ghosts of the future.

THE FIRST EYEFUL of the hill and its immediate perimeter, settling his search next on where the hole in the hump had been burrowed out by a tunnel-boring machine, no doubt, and Bolan wanted to believe the late Freeman's testimony was an accurate account.

It didn't look like much at all, in fact, a brown rolling mass stretching east to west, all of maybe two hundred yards across, seventy feet or so high at its pinnacle. According to Freeman the main entrance was a steel door, now shut, just behind two parked, black-painted eighteen-wheelers. A main corridor, walls supported by thick steel, a single elevator shaft leading to the guts of the place, twenty feet below. Main work area for the specialists, sealed off by decon chambers. A warehouse for the end product, the Hellboxes. Mess hall, sleeping quarters, command central at the far north end of the hill, or so claimed the dead man, shot down by one of his own.

The good news from Bolan's perspective was that the war birds, pylons clearly holding out wings of firepower, were grounded.

The bad news, Bolan saw, were the bobbing heads coming his way, the muzzles of SMGs poking over the edge of a gulley that spined away from his perch on a rocky knoll. They were on the march, still a couple hundred yards but closing.

The heat was on.

Bolan reviewed and assessed. The drive here had eaten up four hours, but other than the one encounter no armed opposition had been sent out to intercept and eliminate. That told Bolan they had chosen to wait for him to make his next move, allow him to wade onto their sacred turf. The soldier had left his SUV behind in what passed as a narrow ravine to the south, heading out on foot, loaded with enough firepower to take on two full-strength platoons. One of the items requested and delivered by Brognola before leaving D.C. was a blacksuit that could be reversed to a brownish-tan. Obviously, the hope he would have blended in as just a part of the desert scenery didn't pan out. Stretched out on his belly, eyes level with the lip of his roost, Bolan made out the other hardforce creeping his way from the northeast. They were going for a pincers lock, looking to close the vise on his flanks, nail the deal before he advanced any farther.

Fair enough.

His combat harness was weighted with grenades, spare clips, the pouches of his brownsuit filled with a stiletto, garrotte, extra magazines for his side arms. The M-16 M-203 was gripped, a full clip in place, a 40 mm hell bomb loaded and ready to fly.

Bolan gave the lay of the land a last look. It wasn't exactly flat in any direction, but there were crags where time and the elements had worn away the topsoil, rolling pockets where cover could be secured on the fly. Here and there, yucca, cactus, tumbleweed and green spiked vegetation poked up from the ground.

All told, as good a place as any to start a small war, he reckoned.

The Executioner slid down the low rise on his belly, taking the M-16 with him. Out of sight, he chose the closest team of three and went off hunting.

It was time to hurl a few more bodies onto the conveyor belt of death. With enough skill, determination and a little bit of luck, Bolan hoped when the dust settled he wasn't stretched out for the buzzards.

THE HOT SEAT had claimed the life of one man already, and before he took the chair Jenkins paused, already knowing exactly why he felt nerves tweaked by a fair amount of paranoia.

So he held his ground outside the falling curtain of light, peering ahead at the five shadows on the deep end of the Room, faces all but obscured by the gloom. It had been one of his soldiers, Merlot, who had been executed here something like three months ago, right before the man would have been rotated out. Dereliction of duty, or so the old man stated after the Glock cracked and the body fell. Seemed Merlot was held accountable for a photojournalist who had somehow heard about the secret base, made the journey here from—of all places—Roswell. Well, Merlot had nodded off on the job, that much was true, hell, it was caught on video. Two chopper loads of hardmen had been flown in at that time to get situated, briefed for the coming tour of duty. The trespasser in question, or so the after-action report went, had actually filmed the crew disembarking, armed to the teeth, of course, the card swiping and code punching to open the gate caught on tape, the whole nine yards that started the snoop's three-hour-plus watch. How all their high-tech surveillance even missed the clown from Roswell coming their way in the first place—while Merlot slept less than thirty feet away—was still a mystery.

So much for state-of-the-art equipment.

Only a few lingering questions remained in Jenkins's mind. It occurred to him maybe the old man had seen Merlot asleep out there, monitoring the whole shabby display from command central, chosen the next course of action, all around, as a warning to the troops, or any civilians, for that matter, who might risk life and limb for a sneak and peek at the compound.

So the old man marshaled up a hit team to go after their wanderer from Roswell. Roused from sleep, Jenkins had led the hunt, quickly tracking the guy with his flying squad of guns to a motel in Tucumcari. When he'd kicked the door down, Jenkins had found the clown squawking up a storm on the phone, presumably sounding the hue and cry about black projects and spook stuff to a pal back in Roswell, even though the guy launched right off into a blubbering fit how he would keep his mouth shut, swearing on his mother's soul. The snoop, Carson or something like that, had frozen in place at the sight of men in black with sound-suppressed submachine guns aimed in his face but kept pouring on the bull how his lips were sealed, guys, once more bringing his late mom into the equation, like she could reach out from the beyond and vouch for his sorry ass. One of Jenkins's soldiers had promptly but gently relieved the snoop of the phone, put it back on its cradle, this mother's pride and joy all but ready to wet himself as he bleated on, don't kill him and such, the usual. The call was soon traced, using the old man's computers, to a girlfriend in Roswell. Not more than two hours later, she was treated to a 9 mm ventilating the same as her squeeze.

And Merlot had undergone a scathing rebuke from the old man before a gunner from Z-Core, fresh off the chopper, had walked right up behind him and put a bullet in his head.

"Please, sit, Mr. Jenkins. Our hours are short, and the days ahead will be full of peril."

The day now was full of peril enough already, he

thought. Then he pinned the old man's voice to a spot, dead center behind the upraised steel table—the jury box, the way he thought of it from his viewpoint—smack between the four mystery guests. A look behind, and he was grateful the door was shut, the area in that direction clear of any of his soldiers. A bank of cameras, monitoring the desert, glowed to his left. Still more light was aimed toward the hot seat, rendering Jenkins pretty much blind to the watching faces.

Jenkins settled in the steel chair, squinting as he adjusted his eyes to the shroud of falling light, and still couldn't get a clear fix on the faces above and beyond.

"This project was conceived a long time ago, Mr. Jenkins," an unfamiliar voice, to the far right, said.

"While you were still winging it, day to day, in a Pakistani prison."

"Wondering if you'd live through the next hour."

"Before an angel of mercy was delivered to you."

"And your future was carved in stone."

From left to right, excluding the old man, he began to nail down each voice, if not the face. A cloud of smoke, white and barely drifting in the fanning glare from the hot seat, and Jenkins saw only the glass of whiskey lifted, vanishing into some murky point where the old man's face was concealed in shadow.

"The world has been changing, and for the worse, for years now," Voice One claimed.

"The project was originally created for one express purpose," Voice Two said.

What the hell was this? he wondered. It sounded as

if they had the script down pat, rehearsed and recited to prior audience, voices bouncing back and forth, the shadow men able to pick up the ball on cue and keep filling in the dialogue.

Voice Three had a deep bass quality to it, a commanding presence, as if it were used to giving orders. "In the event cities across the United States were, in theory, turned into radioactive wastelands by the Russians, these devices were conceived to have one original goal in mind."

"When the other side launched doomsday, they would be planted around the country," Voice Four said. "Packages of nuclear poison. Whatever land still suitable for farming, water supplies still untainted by the first fallout."

"The working premise being the Russians would not wish to annihilate America, coast to coast."

"Rather, cripple us."

"Land their troops."

"Occupation force."

"Of course they would land in biosuits, at first. In time they would make inroads to land where fallout was weakening, as is the nature of radiation."

"It dies."

"Everything dies."

"Thus the Hellbox."

"We intended to contaminate any and every corner of the United States. Spell CONUS."

"Hawaii, Alaska, also."

"If we couldn't have it, they couldn't, either."

"Same thing south of the border. We factored in drifting fallout, wind, blast radius for the thermonuclear megatonnage in the three and four digits, the brunt of it which would fall on military installations, silos, Kansas and Nebraska, D.C., Virginia Beach, San Diego, Cheyenne Mountain...you have the general picture."

"Critical they neutralize our ability to strike back."

"But if it was a limited strike, as we put it to theory, then Mexico and Central and South America would, essentially, still be fertile soil for occupation."

"But the Hellboxes would already be in place."

"We originally planned to build a thousand."

"We knew the number had to be adjusted in the event of our World War Three scenario."

"Of course, the face of the enemy has changed."

"It used to be the Russians."

"The wall has been torn down."

"Now it's the Chinese."

"Or some madman with the money and the will in the Middle East perhaps."

"Times change. And so we've adapted."

"We believe that in a hundred years, the world as you now know it will cease to exist anyway."

"Perhaps, that is, if what we've learned is true."

"Call it an act of God."

"Or the universe simply acting out the natural order of the alpha and the omega."

"NASA has seen it already. So has NORAD."

"SETI was going to go public with it."

"They were quietly persuaded not to."

"Yes, I see the question in your eyes."

"A few million years ago it hit the Gulf of Mexico,

force something in the range of ten billion times the power of what happened to the Japanese. This one will be Hiroshima and Nagasaki combined, if what we've learned is true, in the fifty-billion-plus range, twice over."

"Only this piece of rock is twice the size of Rhode Island."

"We're talking in terms of the force of a hyper-thermonuclear blast."

"Yes, Mr. Jenkins, a comet."

He felt his spine stiffen like a piece of steel, a big freeze gripping his belly, reaching all the way to his head, making him feel faint for a moment. What the hell was he hearing? Mankind was doomed? Was it even true, much less? Why tell him? Or were they throwing curveballs, trying to keep him off balance, smoke screens about the mother of all asteroids, setting him up while they unloaded their real intent? What was next? They knew the truth about Roswell?

"I see the doubt. Believe us. It's all too terribly true."

"However, if our side can forge ahead with an effective SDI—or so-called Star Wars—we can shoot the thing down."

"Of course, a chunk of it might still break the atmosphere."

"Splash into the Pacific maybe."

"Or the Arabian Sea."

"A tidal wave."

"Turn the Arabian Peninsula and the Indian subcontinent into a very large swimming pool."

"He's here. It's started."

For the first time since he'd taken the hot seat, Jenkins heard the old man speak. The freeze was now generated from the shadows, and he knew what was happening before he even looked to the camera bank. A swivel of his head, and Jenkins saw the face of their nameless adversary for the first time. No mistaking, it was their guy.

Their hunter.

That particular camera, he knew, was settled in a narrow gulley to the west where Team One was on the move. It was only a quick look at the eyes, then the M-16 was flaming away on camera.

On cue almost.

And in living red color, no less, as a splash of crimson streaked the monitor.

The Executioner made the interception in a bowl-shaped dip where the fury of floodwaters had deepened the path in that part of the gulley. He knew they were coming, and they probably knew he knew. Far from an easy tag, in terms of Bolan getting the drop on them, but what happened next told the soldier he was worth more alive than dead.

The first man charging over a sawtooth hump in the floor of the gulley balked for a heartbeat at the sudden appearance of their prey. It was long enough for the Executioner to pivot all the way around the corner where a slab of stone had marked a stretched second of prior cover and catch the lead gunner with a 3-round burst to the chest. Number One was flying back, arms wind-milling, losing the long rifle behind a spray of crimson, when numbers two and three broke rank and peeled off to the sides of the bowl.

They were quick, pros splitting up and firing on the fly, but it wasn't bullets they hurled down the path.

The steel net was already riding the air, blossoming open on lead weights, when the Executioner held back on the M-16's trigger, shuffling to the side, out of reach of the trap falling from the sky. Something tugged at his arm, his ears barely able to register the chink of metal on stone to his immediate rear, as Bolan hosed them down with short concentrated bursts of autofire, the racket of his weapon bouncing off the wall, tuning him out to everything next except nailing the enemy. The net hit the area he just vacated on a tinny crunch of steel mesh, the walls on either side of the Executioner bracing the flailing bodies of the gunners as his M-16 chattered on, a blazing lead finger sweeping from one target to the other. Chopped and dropped.

All done for now.

The soldier swiveled his head in both directions, checked his rear, aware he needed to get out of the gulley and keep surging. Three more were on the way, figure 150 to 200 yards out, bearing down. Time enough to note the HK SMGs, still hung in place around the shoulders of his fallen enemies. One look at the small boxes with two metal prongs fastened to their belts, and the logical conclusion was the big shots wanted him strung up, in reasonable shape and singing. It gave Bolan a definite edge, knowing they were out to capture, not kill.

Whoever the brains behind this new angle, well, as far as the Executioner was concerned the hunters were on a fool's errand.

All lined up and marching to their doom. Things looked to be shaping up his way.

He made a decision to backtrack, hug the face of the gulley wall, gambling the other trio would go for an intercept point north, down the gulley. He was wheeling, halfway around, when it glittered in his eyes.

A grim smile pulled at the corner of Bolan's mouth as he tracked the soft whirring clank to its source. The metallic scorpion, a cyclopic black eye protruding out on its shiny dome and aimed Bolan's way, crawled out of a narrow jag in the wall's base. Time was wasting, he knew, but he spared a moment to let the M-16 greet any spectators.

THE DARK GUY with the eyes of death was making a statement, no question. Even the four voices—giving respect where it was clearly, ominously due—ended their scripted routine to watch the show, or what was left, rather, of the opening blood drama. The spider robot-cam shimmied onto the scene just as the last body was pitching, catching a speck of blood on its lens to mark the grim finale. The big guy, decked out in full combat regalia, looked set to roll back in the direction he'd just come from to dust Ambercrombie, Jetson and Paulsen—opting for a backtrack maneuver while Robbins, Shockley and Burns veered north to cut him off, as indicated by another camera—when something like a graveyard smile tugged at the corner of his mouth. Death Eyes turned, instinct, it would appear, putting him eye-to-eye with the spider cam. And Jenkins felt the ice tapping his spine when those eyes stared into the camera, a no-shit look like he'd never seen holding him frozen in his seat, before the muzzle of the M-16 came into view and the guy let the next burst do the talking. The camera blinked out, blinding them to whatever might happen in the gulley.

Like it mattered, Jenkins bitterly mused. His people were out there, dying quick, and more to come. They might as well use a water pistol to try to put out this particular raging wildfire. This badass was good, he was on a tear and he was coming their way.

"We've heard the rumors," Jenkins heard one of them, maybe Voice Three, say, no big deal their world was about to come crashing down.

"Something like this, I understand through the void, happened in Utah recently. Another black project that went belly-up."

"We ran a background with the little available information we had at our disposal, courtesy of our source in Washington."

"And?" The old man, something new, raw in his tone. Fear?

"They call him Belasko."

"And?"

"All the *t*'s are crossed, all the *i*'s dotted."

"Meaning the appropriate ruse has been built to conceal his true identity."

"It would appear so."

None of the cameras showed the badass at the moment, Jenkins figuring he was on the rampage again, either by accident or design skirting away from any surveillance eyes, going for the flank of Team Two. Dammit, he should have been out there! He was on the verge of demanding the old man hand over a radio so he could at the very grim least stay in touch with his troops while monitoring the action when one of the voices cleared his throat.

The stage act, the curtain going up again. It galled him for a second to believe they were more interested in their doomsday spiel and rhetoric about Apocalyptic asteroids and the extinction of life on earth a hundred years from now than the lives of the men under his command. And what the hell did he care what happened to mankind a hundred or so years from now anyway? It wasn't as if he were leaving someone behind to sweat out the unknown tomorrow. He didn't have children—not any that he was aware of—so he couldn't care less if the world ended a hundred or a hundred thousand years from now.

"Now, Mr. Jenkins, as we were saying..."

BEFORE THE SECOND set of hunters knew what hit them, Bolan ended it with a 40 mm thunderbolt that rocked their world. He was rising over the edge of the gulley when he caught them out in the open. They were in a staggered line, three sets of grim eyes focused on the gulley ahead, when Bolan chose his point of impact—a recliner-size boulder—and caressed the M-203's trigger. They were swinging in his direction now, way too late as the 40 mm missile sliced a path between two of them and went off on impact with the rock. The blast took out goons one and two, as anticipated, but the third guy caught a face full of razoring stone bits, grabbing at his eyes, screaming and hopping around before the soldier drilled him in the chest with a 3-round burst of autofire.

Now what?

Advancing on the pool of torn and smoking meat, he gave the tableland leading to the hill a hard search. Snipers? He didn't think so. From where he stood he couldn't discern any decent roost, a crack in the hillside, a hollow where a sniper team could watch the action unfold, choose their moment to let it rip. Besides, they meant to injure him, at worst, as he noted the transparent barrel on the pistol discarded near unfeeling fingers. A steel-tipped tranquilizer dart glistened at Bolan as it mirrored the burning orange eye, which had torqued up the heat to a blistering hundred-plus, he figured. A gas mask caught his eye, then he saw the canisters fixed to their belts. The soldier claimed a mask, attached it to his webbing. The opposition might think themselves full of surprises, but Bolan was ready to counter any move meant to gas him into helpless submission.

As if they could have, anyway.

A fresh clip slapped into the M-16, and Bolan moved back into the gulley, fisting the sweat out of his eyes. Another scorpion cam greeted his descent, and he blasted the thing to sparking ruins, indulging a rare streak of malice. Maybe it was the heat. Maybe it was the glaring uncertainty of what his next move would be that was boiling his blood.

Well, he knew he could *maybe* himself into a serious jam, but second-guessing and looking for reasons to get motivated weren't part of his nature. All he could say was he was going for the black war birds, the tractor trailers and their cargo, next. The Executioner was fired up to make life even more miserable for the watchers hiding inside the hill. As far as Bolan was concerned, they'd picked the wrong day, and most certainly the wrong guy to play games with.

THE ROCK OF ALL AGES streaking from some distant galaxy, on course to plow into earth and send man the way of the dinosaurs, already had Jenkins throwing on the mental brakes. Their thing wasn't about saving mankind from itself, anyway, so why, then, ramble off on weird tangents, even now alluding they did, in fact, know the truth about what happened out here over fifty years ago. He found himself growing more distrustful, suspicious, cynical the longer he sat in the face of their shadows, forced to endure the spiel. They were saying much, but telling him very little, when all he wanted was just the facts.

Then they started tossing around "they," in reference to the economic boom that the previous Administration had very little to do with. "They" filled the shopping malls. "They" fed the great economic monster on Wall Street. "They" fattened to obscene dimensions the bank accounts of the snippy jealous guardians of the culture out in Hollywood, with all their questionable morality and trash "they" passed off as entertainment. At that point, the question had to have hung there in his eyes because Voice Four said, "Sheep. 'They.'"

But, of course. The sheep.

So, now they were gods among mere mortals, steering the course of human history, while "they" were meant to serve, bow and scrape, serve up the cocktails. Or were perhaps just simply in the way, extermination the only saving grave for the sheep.

"A new course must be set."

"It's been tried in the past but failed for any number of reasons."

"Hitler. Stalin."

"Napoleon. The Khans. Alexander."

"There must those who reign. Those who serve. Mankind is divided into ninety-eight percent sheep, two percent shepherd. Peasants and their lords and masters. Nature's way."

"It's a sad fact of human nature that people lie."

"Conspiracies do happen."

"And, perhaps, there really are extraterrestrial biological entities in deep freeze."

"We intend to be the guardians of the future, the architects of a new truth for man."

The voice of authority rolled forth from the shadows. "What we are saying is quite simply the world is about to head into the most perilous time man has ever known. We know. We are about to invent the future. If a man is not with us, then he is against us."

"And if he is against us we have no use for him."

"And no choice."

There it was. Ultimatum time. Some defining, he hoped, of the goal and his role in the mission.

"Do you have any questions, Mr. Jenkins?"

"Yes, sir, I do. First, why are you telling me all of this?"

Before one of them could answer, a flash struck the corner of his eye. Jenkins looked toward the cam bank just in time to see three more of his men go down. Now the badass was winging around grenades from his M-203, the fireball winking out on screen, dust and smoke hovering over three more bodies.

"Impressive."

"That's the old school stuff, gentlemen. Charge the trench, stare it in the eye."

Badass shot out another spider cam.

"The way it used to be done."

"Before smart bombs."

"And cruise missiles."

"The man is one of a kind. What are the chances, do you think, of the man accepting a blank check from us to join the team?"

"Slim to none."

"Less than zero."

"Recruit him? We would stand a better chance winning a fifty-million-dollar state lottery, and with one ticket."

"The eyes told the story. Determined. Been there and back, many times. Honor. Integrity."

"Indeed. We are looking at a one-man juggernaut. God, they don't make them like that anymore, not in this man's army."

Jenkins nearly erupted out of his seat, his blood burning with rage. His men were getting shot to hell and blown to shit, the old man having given a decided edge to the badass with an order that had AFU—all fouled up—written all over it, stem to stern.

"Sir, permission to leave and field a unit to go after the hostile."

"Denied, Mr. Jenkins," the old man said, producing a bottle and pouring another whiskey. "Remain seated."

So he watched the old man hit the button on a small intercom, sipping whiskey, blowing smoke from his cigar. "Brockton?"

"Sir?"

"Proceed. Open the gate. I want my trucks and my choppers cleared from the premises on the double. So much as a scratch on my birds or trucks, I will personally have your head. Understood?"

"Yes, sir!"

Jenkins thought he detected a noticeable lack of enthusiasm in Brockton's affirmative. Who could blame him? he thought.

The old man was about to march a few more out there to the killing field. Bring the badass in, one piece, no shooting to kill. He wished them luck just the same, a false hope they could pull it off. He was beginning to believe he was the only sane individual in the Room.

"Now, Mr. Jenkins, what was your question?"

9

The wall opened, and the first wave of hardmen spilling out from the maw were treated to another burst of Bolan's M-16 autofire.

Hello, and goodbye.

Welcome to the slaughter show, the curtain's up, the demons laughed.

A part of Bolan, even still, cried out from some angry flaming point deep inside, telling him this was a sorry waste of good men.

But gone bad.

No time to mourn what could have been, his ass was on the line.

And falling into enemy hands, alive and steaming just the same, was never an option. There were fates worse than death.

The soldier had already staked out his next point of attack when they came, a dozen shooters in all, guys breaking off right away—pros who had been down the road to hell before—two going down out of the gate as the Executioner zipped them, left to right, with a stitching barrage of 5.56 mm send-offs.

Bolan was forced to drop beneath the edge of the

shallowest point at the far north end of the jagged womb, away from the flying wall of the enemy's lead. They were firing on the fly, HK MP-5 subguns barking in unison, but the steady salvos appeared directed at the earth beyond the soldier's fire point. A blanket of swarming lead kept skidding and whining off the broken ground, almost in Bolan's face, driving him farther down the gulley.

Cover fire so they could advance, he reckoned, gain a toehold up the hill or outflank him. They might be under orders to bag him with no mortal wounds, but a wild bullet didn't listen to any voice of command.

Bolan fell a few more yards down the hole. When he risked a look up and over, he found a few of the gunners, sweeping subgun fire as they surged on, had obviously been ordered to secure the transport. Meaning get it the hell out of there.

Engines were grinding to life, masked somewhat by the enemy's SMG pounding, then Bolan saw a few runners bounding into the bellies of the flying beasts. The M-203 was filled, good to go, but if he pulled off the coming stunt he would dwindle his supply of hell bombs.

What the hell, he figured, felt himself turning as cold as ice inside.

This was shit city, overcrowded by savages with something to hide, innocents to burn.

He wasn't there anymore, fighting for his life, hell-bent on unraveling some conspiracy about silent high-tech mass murder because he had nothing better to do.

It was hitting the fan. They'd called him out, someone believing they knew Justice had smelled out the stink, marching him, then, into the guns.

The Executioner was nobody's chump.

No mistake, the enemy wasn't about to leave here, by truck or chopper or on foot. Unless, of course, it was on his terms.

Down and out for good.

THE SHADOWS TALKED ON in that condescending tone, as if he were beneath them, as if it were an honor for him to be in their presence.

It was all Jenkins could do to keep from shouting out loud—in a bellow of righteous anger—the running list of questions burning up his thoughts. They took their sweet time getting to the bottom line—whatever that was—and as a war was in full swing on camera, the biggest problem he'd seen in recent or distant memory, for that matter, damn near perched on their doorstep. A human hawk was swooping and grabbing and tearing it up like he knew the drill so well it was just another day at the office.

If he hadn't seen it with his own eyes, Jenkins would have said later it was just some other guy's booze-drenched tall tale, most likely fabricated to cover his deficiencies and lack of stones in the face of fire.

The reality of his moment, though, the truth so shocking, so sobering, in fact, it made him wonder what really waited in the unknown of the great beyond.

"A certain situation has developed in a foreign country."

"Men who work for us have been in place for some time now."

"A buyer for several of the devices has been groomed. Those devices are now to be delivered."

"A handsome sum of money waiting for all of us on the other end."

"And how do I fit in?"

There. He'd said it, and gave himself a silent pat on the back, especially when he felt the chill blowing his way from the shadows.

The old man spoke for the group when the four shadows held a collective silence. Jenkins wished to God he could see their faces, imagined them stumped, this peasant-soldier daring to raise a voice in question, confronting the gods.

Kiss my ass, gentlemen. Do time, hard time. Then come and talk to me.

"There will be a blank check for you at the successful conclusion of the next step, should you decide to accept. A blank check where you can write in your own price."

"To do what? Sir."

"Oversee the transaction. With myself along for the event, of course. With six specialists in tow, to be handed over to the buyer."

"Who is, sir?"

"His identity is of no real importance to you at this time."

"Sir, should I accept, with all due respect, I believe I would be the best judge of that."

The whiskey glass was raised, vanished, then lowered into the murky light. A fresh smoke cloud blew from the shadows. "Your answer, then?"

What was he going to say? No? Refusal could be viewed by the old man as ingratitude, at best, insubordination, at its grimmest verdict. Jenkins was under no illusions that he was exempt from suffering the same penalty as the puddle of bloody gristle they'd recently left behind for the scavengers. He was on their payroll. They knew he knew that, and any prospects for employment outside the project were probably next to zero. They owned him. They had planned this moment for a long time. The lenders had made him their servant. That insight alone sunk an annoying weight in his belly. If they could so skillfully maneuver his destiny, then putting an abrupt end to this preordained journey would be easy as snapping their fingers. Kiss off, hell, no, he wouldn't go, and he was certain the order would be given as soon as he was walking out the door. One of his own men even, coming up behind, putting one in the back of his head.

Jenkins swallowed, cleared his throat, hoped his attempt at regaining composure passed the test. "Yes, sir. I accept. Now, can someone please answer my questions?"

Voice Two volunteered. "He is an Iranian fundamentalist."

"Translation," Jenkins said, frustration and confusion somehow fueling a new fire in his blood, now that he'd spoken up, made inroads through the shadows. "He's a terrorist."

"You know the saying, Mr. Jenkins?"

"One man's terrorist is another man's freedom fighter. I've heard it. I'm listening."

Sounding ballsy. Good. Hold that tone.

"He came from a wealthy family with powerful connections in Tehran."

"Oil money. Lots of oil money. Tons, in fact. Cash. Paper manna from Allah."

"Did it ever bother you, if you cared to think about it, how some drifters on camelback just happened to be sitting on a sea of dead dinosaurs—translate fossil fuel."

"Translate gasoline."

"Your SUV."

"TWA."

"Hertz."

"The backbone of Western economy and power."

"Western genius erecting the oil fields, the whole wherewithal to land OPEC on the throne."

"Energy."

"The destiny."

"The equation."

"The one equalizer that makes them think we should behold them in the blinding light."

"The Iranian is now in hiding. No Paul on the way to Damascus there."

"Believed to have bridged some gap to a particular Saudi fundamentalist also in hiding."

"Bin Laden?"

"The same. Yes."

"Wait a second. You're telling me..."

"Yes."

"You've accepted."

"And Raven will be along, don't forget."

"The deal of the new century, the one that will further our agenda, will happen in Afghanistan."

The reconsideration had to have shown, a neon sign, because Jenkins heard the voice of authority say, "Is that a problem?"

"You've been in countries nearly equal in danger."

And "nearly," he thought, was the operative word. Afghanistan.

He might as well ride that UFO to Mars. He'd never been there, the barren anus of Baluchistan as close as he got before getting nailed with a truckload of raw opium, but he knew a few men in his line of work who had that particular grim displeasure. And the lucky ones who made it out, he recalled, the war dogs stating it with nerves barely soothed by a gallon or two of whiskey, that the place defined hell on Earth.

In the next moment, another brighter flash flared from the camera bank in the corner of his eye. He heard the old man snarl a string of curses, using creative obscenity that would have done some rapper proud, but Jenkins was already homed in on the latest wave of destruction on their doorstep, pretty much deaf to everything except the next hammering of his heartbeat in eardrums, the runaway pulsing of his blood. One, then two fireballs hammered near the front gate. The angle of the camera caught Blackbird One in liftoff, five or so feet off the ground, then it was lit up by a fireball, a miniversion, perhaps, of that rock of ages destined to extinguish life on Earth the shadows spoke of, before the force of blast number two sent it crashing into the side of the hill. Jenkins felt the shock waves ripple across the floor under his feet, saw two more surveillance eyes blinking out as the doomed chopper came apart to riddle the hillside—and their doorstep—with yet more evidence there was no room for second place in the cosmos.

Oh, this was rich, he thought. He couldn't help but

wonder if some divine warning had just come attached to his new package deal, slated for halfway around the world, an Iranian, and Taliban thugs hungry to irradiate the infidels. The way it was shaping up out there, he figured he'd be lucky to even see the living hell that was Afghanistan.

BOLAN DUMPED the 40 mm fireball inside the fuselage of demon bird one. He then stuffed the M-203 with an incendiary round, sighted, then squeezed again.

The chopper almost made it off the ground, despite the fireworks ripping out its guts, Bolan tipping a mental salute to the tenacity of the flyboys trying to save the day.

Even the devil deserved his due, Bolan guessed, but that didn't mean slack time or showing sympathy when evil meant to advance itself and eat up the innocent.

He spared a moment, braving the ricochets sparking off the tableland ahead, whizzing past out of range as he judged their tracking and waited it out while the chopper blew into a fireball so bright it made him turn away, wincing.

Then the bird lost it all as it slammed into the hillside just above the grand opening. Fuel ignited, ammo caught the searing heat and the raging touch of the initial blast, and it was gone for good.

The fire cloud sent two hardmen riding across the tableland. One of them hit the deck a few feet away from Bolan, moaning, and he relieved the guy of his misery with a quick 3-round burst to the face.

Okay. Assume Freeman was telling the truth, he thought. A force of thirty, now shaved by less than half, the headshed sending them out with orders to capture.

Easy pickings from there on?

Hardly.

Bolan swung his M-16 around, hit the trigger and rattled off a stream of 5.56 mm steel hornets, stung another gunner as he beelined a path, charging for a course that would have nearly planted him on top of the soldier's flank. The men flopped to the hillside, the parched soil drinking up a narrow run of crimson.

The Executioner launched himself into a running leap out of the gulley, slapping home a fresh magazine, cocked and locked.

A few survivors were scurrying away from the plunging wreckage, racing out of the smoke and fire, voices hurling panic, confusion and anger his way.

Bolan marched on.

10

Two human torches flared before a camera, there then gone, dropped out of sight from the monitor, presumably the badass sparing some mercy rounds to silence what he could only imagine were blood-curdling shrieks of pure agony. Jenkins was grateful the sound was off, only the horror show playing out before their eyes was somehow made worse still by the silence on-screen, not to mention the mere sight of a bunch of dead men filling up the monitors was wreaking havoc on his nerves. An icy chill walked down his spine.

Hell on Earth or whatever, Afghanistan was looking better by the minute.

Voice One betrayed the first sign the group's nerve was cracking. "How long did you say before the other units from Z-Core arrive?"

"They should be landing in thirty minutes," the old man answered. "They've already been briefed on the situation here."

An eternity, Jenkins thought, and it was news to him that the old man was bringing in the cavalry.

"Here are the basics, Mr. Jenkins," Voice Three said. "You will be flying from here shortly with whatever still stands of Z-Core. A C-130 Hercules will be loaded up with the devices, our human cargo, the specialists."

The shadow made it sound like one big family picnic, he thought.

"It has been arranged through certain channels the flight is a mission of mercy to a drought-plague area in Pakistan."

"Food, water, medical supplies."

"A team of engineers flown in to help the Pakistanis build a dam, a hydroelectric plant."

"Water refinery."

"The ruse, of course, is that this is a Red Cross operation."

"Helping the Pakistani masses regain a sense of dignity and humanity with our show of charity. They've been promised compensation in the form of one Hellbox."

"The late major was instrumental in helping our side get this far."

"Only there were certain individuals in the ISI who didn't want to see the devices fall into his hands."

"So his sudden passing will not be mourned."

"I'll fill you in more once we're in the air," the old man said. "For now, Mr. Jenkins, I want you to go outside and take care of that problem."

If he wasn't sure he'd heard that right, it was because Jenkins felt a cold touch of fear on his heart.

"Step up here," the old man said. "My previous orders stand. You will use nonlethal force," he added, and Jenkins saw the plastic pistol with a tranquilizer dart in its see-through barrel.

BOLAN SPARED the trucks out of basic suspicion they were loaded with radioactive poison. He had no biosuit at this point, and he didn't need to place himself under anymore stress than he already had by traipsing around in a radiated hotbed.

The soldier was under plenty enough duress as things stood. And there were other ways to take down the trucks without resorting to more smash and burn.

Such as unloading a gale force of M-16 autofire on the drivers.

The Executioner swung his M-16 toward the cabs of the black tractor trailers. One driver for each cab, grim faces staring back as they ground gears and lurched their rolling beasts of burden forward, and Bolan cut loose. Downrange, advancing, he hosed the closest windshield, blowing in the glass, obliterating the face behind the wheel as he followed through, holding back the trigger. A check of the kill zone near the front entrance, a few stragglers pulling themselves standing, and he found he was blessed with a piece of good fortune.

Before the second chopper could lift off, a sheet of wreckage floated down and plowed into the tail rotor. Guys were screaming like there was no tomorrow, bumping into each other in some bizarre Laurel and Hardy act that was hardly a slapstick routine under the circumstances. Bolan was running, clearing ground zero. He didn't see what happened next but heard the screech of metal as the doomed chopper hammered the ground, perhaps flipped on its side from the sound of all the tearing and wrenching on the other side of the rig.

The soldier secured cover down the side of the unmanned rig, firing from the hip at driver number two, scoring an encore performance, when the chopper blew. He had to figure the bird's fuel tank was topped out, judging by the earsplitting roar of thunder, the dazzling blaze he felt scorch his face. He figured it knifed down on its main rotor following its rollover, internal wreckage beating up the inner workings, sparking off the big bang.

Whatever, he was moving on, searching for fresh targets. He didn't have to look far, wait long. Another 30-round clip rammed home in the assault rifle, he charged between the giant hearses, came out the other side shooting. Two stragglers were diced to bloody ribbons by the soldier's long burst, spinning away in opposite dueling pirouettes. Number three went for broke, shouting a curse that told Bolan whoever issued his nonlethal orders could take this job and shove it. The Executioner's grim handiwork bore out another stroke of good fortune. A falling slab of wreckage knocked off Mr. Spite's aim, his line of autofire snapping the air beside Bolan's ear. A brief round of cursing as the falling sky shoved him to his knees, and Bolan threw the bitterness back in his face, slashing his chest with a marching core of 5.56 mm doom, dumping the guy in the ranks of the permanently unemployed.

Death clause in his contract.

A list of harsh smells clawed his senses—blood and spilled guts, toasting flesh and burning fuel, emptied bladders and bowels. The heat was so intense, Bolan was soaked in sweat by the time he was ready to make his move to penetrate the compound.

He was wondering if the tear gas would ever enter the picture when some psychic hardman, masked and directing a wild spray of subgun fire that chased Bolan to cover behind a mound of jagged chopper trash, barreled out the opening and pitched the canister. It was already hissing, spewing noxious fumes, bouncing off the ground, when Bolan tugged on his mask.

Two more masked shooters charged out of the hole, broke off to the side, blanketed Bolan's cover with a wall of lead. And what happened next was a rare oversight on the soldier's part. In his world, where sudden death was the order of the day, even the briefest of mental lapses was all it took, and he was tagged.

Bolan knew what the bee sting on his leg meant before he even looked.

The only thing he could figure was the guy had taken another way out, an emergency tunnel that cut through the hill to Bolan's right where the shooter had gained a vantage point, high enough up the hill and to his blind side to pull it off. It didn't matter anymore, the curtain was already dropping on this deadly gig as Bolan looked down where the needle was impaled in his thigh. He'd left his blind side open not more than a few seconds, and now he could already feel his limbs growing heavy, swelling, it seemed, with what he could only imagine as something like rapidly drying cement weighting him down. He was raising the assault rifle, but the shooters were going in and out of focus as nausea ballooned inside his head and gut. The soldier toppled, felt his back slam earth, the sun in his eyes for a brief moment, then the sky went black.

"NICE WORK, Mr. Jenkins. Assume a bonus will be added to your next check before we conclude our final business and you've earned that fat payday we mentioned."

"He's coming around, sir. I only shot him with a low dose."

"It's been nearly ninety minutes already. Slap him."

"No need for all that. The man's a soldier. Let's show a little respect," someone said, Bolan hearing a new voice coming at him from some distant horizon.

Bolan pried open the lead weights that were his eyelids. The white light stabbed him in the eyes, forcing him to squint. The good news, of course, was that he was still alive. The bad news was obvious. He was a prisoner, disarmed. What was next? Truth serum? Torture? Then a bullet to his head?

"I'm called Raven."

The soldier's brain felt stuffed with cotton. He thought at first he was still paralyzed by the drug, immobile, then noted the ropes lashed around his arms. He was in some sort of conference room or maybe command center. He noted a bank of cameras off to the side. Framed in the beam of light it was difficult, even as the fog cleared in his eyes, to make out the faces of the shadows sitting in front and above on some sort of long raised table. A look to his right, and he found they'd heaped his war bag, weapons and gear displayed like trophies.

"Don't worry, Special Agent Belasko of the Justice Department, you'll be able to take everything with you once you leave here. As if you'll really be needing it."

"So, I'm free to go," Bolan said, and sounded a grim chuckle. "That's real sporting of you."

"Not quite. You'll be taking a little journey with us. Call it a vacation from all your problems, if you will."

"You don't strike me as the kind to lay around a beach all day, sipping drinks with little umbrellas in them."

"I suppose it would be a colossal waste of time to attempt to get you tell us who you really are."

"You saw the ID wallet."

"And our background check on your Belasko cover holds, as far as your ruse goes."

"So, what's your 'ruse'?"

"Where we're going next, it's simply called 'show me the money.'"

"The Hellboxes, you mean. You've put them on the auction block."

He assumed the shadow doing all the talking was the one who identified himself as Raven. "Specifically, the devices will be sold to an Iranian, presently wanted by our side for a long list of terrorist acts. The usual stuff. Embassies and planes going up in a flaming holocaust. A car bomb now and then in Tel Aviv, just to show the Israelis he's still thinking about them. You know maybe to whom I refer?"

Between missions, Bolan always scanned the target files at Stony Man. He liked to know who was doing what and where, out there in the world of bad guys he might someday go hunting for. The Iranian in question leaped to Bolan's mind. Jabik Kahmujouti. Inherited billions in oil money from his father. Usually marched off lackeys to do the dirty jobs for him against the Great Satan, but the fingers always pointed back his way. The Iranian was more into sponsorship, arranging weapons deliveries to the troops, mapping out the strategy for the next round of slaughter. A nasty piece of work just the same. It was a well-known fact the FBI, Interpol, the CIA were prowling for him. Only Kahmujouti had been granted refuge in Afghanistan. The word was he'd joined his fanatic's hand with the other most wanted terrorist, Bin Laden.

"Afghanistan's not exactly in my vacation plans."

"Maybe you'll learn to like it. So much, you might wish to spend your final days there. You see, someone back east has been digging around in our affairs. Clever bastards, they hack into certain mainframes, but before anybody can pin them down, they've thrown up the fire wall. You wouldn't by chance know who they are, would you?"

He did, of course, but Bolan would take that bullet to the brain before he'd betray the Farm.

"I never was much on all that computer jazz."

"Right," the voice said. "I've seen your work. You're old school. Let the real fighting, the killing do all the talking for you."

Bolan felt a presence moving behind him. A shadow broke into the light, a dark man in black stepping in front of Bolan.

"I believe you've already met Mr. Poe?"

Bolan watched as Poe stopped in the light. If his hands weren't tied down, the soldier knew he'd rip the smirk right off the guy's lips with his fingers, then take some degree of pleasure owed him when he choked the life out of the man.

"If I thought you'd be a good soldier boy, I'd untie you, shake your hand for getting this far. Quite amazing what you did." Poe took a gold case from inside his jacket, snapped it open and shook free a cigarette. When he had it fired up and blew some smoke Bolan's way, the wolf's grin came back. "You see, for a long time now, our people have been hearing these fantastic tales of some lone troubleshooter who seems to leave dead bodies behind wherever he goes. Always bad guys, terrorists, drug dealers, like that, folks who are pretty much beyond the reach of legitimate law enforcement. Sometimes he's been known to work with the FBI. Sometimes the DEA, the CIA."

Poe shrugged, smoked, but lost the smile. "A few people of means and power are stirred up in high places, some rumors floating around that maybe Hal Brognola is running some black ops gig out of the Justice Department."

Bolan returned Poe's look with a wry grin. "Hey, I'm just your average G-man, fella. No more, no less."

"Barking up the wrong tree, that it?"

"Let's just say you're so far out there in the upper deck, not even a tape measure McGwire or Sosa shot would reach you."

"Okay. I'll let you blow the smoke in my face for now," he said, hit the butt hard and launched a cloud into the light. "So, how does it all play from here?" Bolan asked. "Since we're being friendly and all and I don't see any thumbscrews yet."

Poe stepped away from the light. "How it's going to work, troubleshooter, is like this. A deal has been in place with the Iranian for long, nervous weeks now while the logistics were nailed down and the proper wheels were greased. We've got the window of opportunity open. Only your guy, Brognola, sends you to a cutout who comes to me. The monkey wrench—you."

The big Fed's choice of contacts was definitely something Bolan intended to hash over with Brognola, assuming, of course, he even lived through the next few hours. It happened like that, though, Brognola forced to deal in a world that wore masks, maintained secret agendas, sharpening their treacherous blade to stick it in somebody's back. He wasn't laying the blame for his present crisis at his friend's doorstep by any means. The truth was actually quite the opposite. The present danger of this conspiracy had been rooted out, thanks to Brognola's quiet urging. Without that, Bolan would still be at the Farm, waiting for that clear and present danger he could have sunk his teeth into. Such was the game whenever he walked among the shadows. To some larger extent timing had proved everything. His present enemies—whoever they really were—had always been out there, doing whatever they did, dreaming up and engineering this Hellbox scenario. Bolan determined that since they weren't about to outright kill him, well, where there was hope an answer would be provided.

A way out, to jump-start the ass kicking again.

"Put him under. Enough to hold him for a good while."

Poe was back in Bolan's face, holding out a hypodermic needle.

"We'll talk about your future on the plane ride. Right now, this place is set to go up soon, and getting turned into nothing more than a shadow on the ground by a nuclear explosion isn't my idea of that day at the beach you mentioned. There will be the usual quiet squawking, NORAD wondering what the hell when we leave behind a crater, thanks to something in the neighborhood of ten kilotons."

Even if he could have thought up some clever one-liner meant to put the fear of the devil into Poe, Bolan would have skipped it. He let the eyes say it all as he held Poe's stare—Bolan would even the score.

11

The next time he dredged himself out of limbo and into the waking shroud was far worse than when he came around in the chair. Splitting headache, cotton mouth, sluggish limbs and a sick knot in his belly aside, climbing out of a drug-induced semicomatose state was the least of his concerns. In due course the cloud would filter itself out of his system.

Survival became top priority. Escape, too, to get back on track and crush the enemy. At the moment the odds of striking back anytime soon weren't even on the board, all the dice, weighted and assured to roll up their way, firmly in their hands.

Finding himself squeezed in like a human cannonball, knees drawn to his chest, the Executioner saw he was locked in some kind of holding cell. His prison was clearly designed to create discomfort and a crushing sense of claustrophobia, his captors showing off a sadistic streak perhaps. He found he was scrunched in a steel cylinder not much wider than a torpedo chute. A yellow eye glowed overhead, and he could be sure his watchers knew he was just now coming back to the land of the living. He caught the soft hiss of air being piped in, focused on long deep intakes of oxygen. It took a good minute or more before he forced enough of the narcotic's clutch from the pulsing gel of his brain to allow him to start thinking straight.

No sound beyond the cylinder. No way to tell time. Poe had shot him up with enough juice to put him under for a good while. Could have been six hours or two days. He rolled his head on a neck that felt barely held onto his shoulders by rubbery muscle. He flexed his fingers, felt the burning stiffness in his hands, clenched his fists, knuckles popping like firecrackers in the cramped womb of the chute.

Before his capture he'd been running on empty, virtually no food or water, and with the desert heat depleting his body's natural water supply, there was no pressure on his bladder. Scratch one minor inconvenience. His parched mouth was dry and raw as some of that sunbaked earth he'd left behind—whether from the drug or dehydration or a combination of both—and a simple gulp of tepid canteen water would have been welcomed as a blessing. Any man in captivity, he knew, having been down this road before, could find himself longing for the simple creature comforts the free man had at his whim, might take for granted....

Stow it. Willpower alone had guided the soldier beyond his basic need for food and water before. Deprivation came with the turf, always had, and there was something to be said, he knew, for mind over matter.

From there on, Bolan knew very little about his situation was guaranteed except the threat of death at the hands of his captors. So, he would take his dilemma one small step at a time, ride it out, look for an opening, strike back when the narrowest window of opportunity cracked. They were keeping him alive for a reason, and that was an A-plus on his scorecard.

A couple of guesses crossed his thoughts in that regard. Maybe he was a bargaining chip, the conspirators stewing in worry they could find themselves dogged by armed hunters like himself or tracked by high-tech or through cyberspace, or loose lips flapping in the corridors of Washington officialdom eventually pointing the sword of Opus Damocles their way. Bolan couldn't say for sure, but the enemy had already thrown around their suspicions that Hal Brognola was more than he claimed to be, at least in the public spectrum of bureaucracy. Or perhaps Bolan was a pawn, meant to get moved around until they had Brognola maneuvered into a corner. No chance of that happening—the soldier had more than a few secrets of his own, and he would take them to the grave, if forced to. And setting Brognola up for Poe and the shadow men to take a closer look, presumably at the business end of their guns, would never happen, either, not if Bolan had anything to say about it.

The other hunch was they wanted to pick his brain, find out who he really was beyond the Belasko charade. And do what? Recruit him? His first impression was they seemed anxious to hire a few good men, and he was just the kind of force of one they'd been searching for. Fat chance he'd ever jump ship, for money or any other worldly incentive. The notion they wanted to hire him as a shooter also struck him as bordering ridiculous, the opposition bringing him onboard after he had shot at and blown up at least half of a full platoon of their Z-Core. But stranger things had happened. Maybe the big shots had meant to thin the ranks of malcontents, substandard soldiers, or simply cut back on their black payroll, using his lethal skills to provide the answers for them. That didn't quite fly, at least not in strict military terms, where loyalty and teamwork and watching the other guy's back counted for something. But he couldn't be certain of anything right then, as he was fully plunged into the abyss of their shadow world. So, then, if he wouldn't become their pawn, soldier or songbird, where did he fit into their equation?

He breathed deeply to clean out his system, and soon his mind was sharpening to review and assess. Depending on how long he'd been out, and with no way to contact Brognola, he knew the big Fed was probably pushed to a frantic threshold. Bolan knew the man wouldn't sleep, much less enjoy a moment's peace until he knew the score on the soldier's end one way or another. The satlink had a homing device, something in the way a transponder worked on an aircraft. But Bolan had to turn it on if the signal was to get bounced to a satellite and back to Stony Man Farm. So Bolan was on his own, cut off from resources, intel, the whole works of aid and assistance. His adopted family of warriors and cyber sleuths would just have to hang in there, wait until he resurfaced. The waiting game, as he marched toward uncertain fate, was familiar ground for them, anyway. Friends just the same, they were all pros, knew and accepted the risks, grimly aware that someday, somewhere he might pay the ultimate price.

The Hellboxes and an Iranian terrorist buyer. Afghanistan. Bolan was no stranger to that part of the world, but in recent years new heights of anger toward the West had rocketed through the Islamic stratosphere of their jihad, acted out by way of rejuvenated hatred of anything not descended of Muslim blood. These days, those feelings were vented by certain Islamic fundamentalist honchos who took asylum in mountain strongholds of the Hindu Kush—Hindu Killer in the native tongue of Pushtu and Dari or its varied dialects closely related to Farsi—or trained whole armies of fanatics in some desert fortress, sending out the killing squads to distant lands to do their butcher work while they reaped the blood glory of their cannibalistic ideals from behind the lines. Bin Laden may have grabbed world headlines, but a few other savages had staked out turf there, buying the mujahadeen, greasing Taliban rebels, bearing smuggled weapons as gifts to fuel to the jihad fervor. Like Kahmujouti.

The basics, for starters, Bolan thought, on the next destination, assuming the enemy had told him the truth. The country, roughly the size of the state of Texas, was locked in by Iran, Pakistan, the Russian splinter states of Turkmenistan, Uzbekistan, Tajikistan to the north, with a narrow mountain corridor to an occupied strip to the far east edge to neighboring China, called the Wakhan. There the Red Army maintained its watchdog post on India, Pakistan and the Afghans, Beijing biding its own time, perhaps, maybe waiting for the missiles to start flying as Pakistan and India pushed the button to nuclear Armageddon, then marching in to claim whatever was left in the glowing ashes. Could be the Chinese, if they caught wind of the Hellbox deal, would want to cut themselves in for a piece of the action.

Afghanistan. Hard country from border to border in every sense, where fierce warriors tended to shoot outsiders on sight and their women were kept veiled head to toe. Historically the country was a highway of conquerors since the time of Alexander, the Mongols, the Russians the latest in a long line of wannabe occupation, driven out when they realized these folks were serious about their freedom and no amount of gassing them from above was about to bring them to their knees. And it was home—or refuge—to rebels, thieves, opium warlords, every ilk and shade of cutthroat and criminal who had the money to buy whatever his version of peace of mind.

Lately the Taliban had shot to the front of the savage herd, recent arrivals on the scene, hyenas circling the old lion, instinctively aware nature was looking to change the dying guard; it just took a brazen show of strength to bring down the tired king of the jungle. Western news pretty much made the Taliban look like a ragtag band of armed hooligans, desperately poor, angered that their collective voice was muted by the ruling body in Kabul. The truth was that they were Pathan warriors, many of whom had been blooded during the brutal Soviet invasion. The ones who survived ten years of getting kicked in the teeth by the Russians were now spurred on by shooting victories against the Afghan army. The Taliban had grabbed up something like forty percent of the Pathan—or Pushtun as it was sometimes called—branching out to gain strangleholds on big chunks of real estate in nine of the other thirty Afghan provinces. Bottom line, Bolan knew, the power of the gun ruled the day.

He heard a click behind his head, a snick as the cylinder parted. He nearly fell on his back but reached out and grabbed the edge, steadied himself.

"Let's talk."

Poe. A bone in his knee cracked as Bolan hefted himself to his feet, squeezed through the narrow opening. The mist was cleared from his eyes. Bolan took a long moment to get his bearings, flex his arms, work out the kinks and stiffness.

"We're nine miles high, Belasko," Poe said, taking a step back, his hand filled with a Beretta 92-F. "Get froggy on us...well, I don't think I need to tell you what a bullet hole in the cabin would do. Human icicles, but we'd all die suffocating before we turned to ice."

A green hue hung over the cabin, and Bolan held his ground for another moment, listening to a four-man team as they talked into their throat mikes, watching the screens of their monitors. Okay, he was on board some classified military flight, probably a Gulfstream jet or some variation. Windows shut, he couldn't tell if it was night or day. "You had a nice long nap. Don't trouble yourself with a bunch of questions I don't care to answer. Such as how long? Where are we? What's the deal?"

"We'll be landing soon enough."

Bolan looked toward the white-haired man facing him from a leather-lined seat amidships. The soldier caught a whiff of whiskey, peered through the cigar smoke and found another timeless but hard face that nearly matched the ageless wonder who'd set him up. Beyond the eyes that had seen a hundred lifetimes, it was almost impossible to get a fix on the white-haired man's years. Poe and the white-haired man, Bolan recognizing his voice as the one who called himself Raven, seemed to have the logistics figured out, all bases covered. But prior experience in shadow games had shown the soldier where there was enough money, clout and determination, enough deceit, lies and manipulation throwing up smoke screens, anything was possible. The brief snatches he caught from the control group up front told Bolan they were handing off clearance codes to whoever was on the receiving end. Maybe a pilot in an F-16 or the admiral of some U.S. fleet wondering why his airspace was suddenly broached by unidentified aircraft.

"Mr. Rogers, has the situation been taken care of?" Raven called over his shoulder.

"Affirmative, sir. We're clear."

"Then I anticipate smooth sailing all the way from here on," Raven said, looking at Bolan, as if saying that for his benefit. "Grab a seat, Belasko."

Bolan settled into the cushioned seat across from Raven. He was looking across the aisle at a grizzled face in buzz cut when Raven introduced the hardman as Mr. Jenkins, who kept an HK MP-5 subgun cradled in his lap, eyes telling Bolan he had no problem using the SMG, even if it meant risking suicide at nine miles above the planet. And two more gunners with weapons stood near the cockpit doorway, watching Bolan. Poe claimed a seat directly opposite the soldier.

"There's water in that thermos," Raven said, nodding at a shelf fixed to the cabin wall beside Bolan. "Unless you'd like some whiskey. You've been cooped up for a long time. Maybe a slug or two to ease the stiffness."

"I'll stick with the water."

Bolan took the thermos, uncapped it and took a deep, slow gulp, felt their stares all around, measuring him, wondering. The cool liquid seemed to fill his belly with a warm glow, but it certainly revived more strength, quickly cutting away the sludge in his limbs. It crossed his mind to reach out and grab Raven by the throat, a hostage in his clutches to force the issue. Suicide, of course, unless they shot him with another dart.

"Let's do this like gentlemen, Belasko—or whoever you really are. We're all professionals," Raven said. "I'm thinking you knew those trucks were off-limits to the bigger fireworks."

"Good you didn't damage the cargo," Poe said.

"Not only were six boxes on board, but there was also three tons of radioactive waste. Mostly Pu-239."

"It would have been quite messy," Poe added.

"Most of it came to us through some friends at Los Alamos, in case you were wondering," Raven said. "The waste is burned off in the reactor incinerators.... Well, I'll spare you the technical side of things. It appears the Iranian wants us to set up shop in a country yet to be determined. Word is he thinks part of the deal is our specialists will show him how to convert the boxes into a nuclear device, which it already is, but the buyer wants instant gratification, so to speak."

"Could pose a problem when we land," Poe said. "It wasn't part of the original deal."

"I hope we can avoid the matter of a shooting war when we land," Raven replied, hit the whiskey then his stogie. "I would like to enlist your services. I am prepared to offer you a flat two million dollars."

"Just to help watch our backs. Nothing more, unless you want to stay on."

Bolan looked around, caught Jenkins's eye for a second, the man turning away. Obviously one of Raven's soldiers resented the idea of the recruitment strategy.

"Should you decline, and I suspect you will," the white-haired man said, "then I will hold on to you for a while. Make sure no other problems find their way to our doorstep. I'm thinking you're a valuable asset to somebody. I'm thinking your continued existence might provide me some leverage when I resume the business of manufacturing the device."

"It was unfortunate we had to blow up all we'd worked so hard to create," Poe said. "It was already designed that way, however. Bail out. Set up shop elsewhere. Your rampage didn't help. Disposal of evidence was necessary. Naturally we have friends in high places who will provide the necessary cover. FEMA will make a show of investigating the crater we left behind in New Mexico. None of this, of course, will ever see the headlines or CNN."

Bolan downed another mouthful of water. "You people seem to have all the answers. I don't see where you need me."

"I'll take that as you declining my offer?" Raven said.

"Thanks for the water," Bolan stated.

"Then you're living on my clock. Stolen time."

"I've been there before."

The white-haired man puffed his cigar, studied Bolan behind the smoke. "Well, you didn't disappoint me. If you'd said yes, I would have chuckled in your face."

"Then why bother?"

"Maybe I just like the game."

"So, I'm good for now until your six is secured."

"You could put it like that, yes. Now, do you walk back in there on your own? Or would you like some help?"

"I'll manage."

Four weapons sprang up as Bolan stood. Poe was on his feet, backing down the aisle, Beretta aimed at Bolan's chest.

"They'll risk it, sir," Raven said. "One well-placed bullet may not puncture the cabin. Maybe just one to the leg, leave you penned up to bleed out."

One last sip of water, heaving a breath, aware he'd never reach the first shooter in time even if he was inclined to risk it all, and Bolan dumped the thermos on his vacated chair. Slowly, the soldier walked back, squeezed into the chute. He turned in time to see Poe lift a remote box, tap a button and close the door from a safe distance.

TWO HOURS EARLIER, by his rough mental calculation, Bolan had caught the voices raised in what sounded like a heated discussion. The steel enclosure muffled the words, but somebody out there had a problem with something or somebody. Small hope, then, that maybe the enemy was on the verge of infighting, nerve cracking as they closed on Afghanistan, the big deal on the other end sounding as if their Iranian buyer was issuing new demands. New stakes had been thrown into the game. One guy wanted more than his already agreed-upon slice of the pie. Standard fare when dealing with savages, but Bolan saw trouble ahead for the conspirators. And with a potential shooting war erupting, Westerners riding in on fanatic Islam soil prepared to hand over a prototype instrument of mass destruction for whatever the going rate. What was to stop the Iranian from taking what he wanted while the conspirators stood there, facing down perhaps an army of fundamentalists? Nothing. Unless they had some contingency plan. But what? Possibly a backpack nuke brought along to up the ante? Or threaten to set it off, ruin the whole deal for everyone concerned if the conspirators found themselves cornered?

Time slogged on, minute by agonizing minute, for the soldier.

Bolan kept a running mental gauge of time as best he could. Figure another five hours, and he had felt the jet's wheels touch down. After stopping, not more than fifteen minutes passed, and they were wheels up again. Since no one volunteered to inform him how long he'd been dropped into his forced nap, and since Poe made it clear not to bother to ask, there was no way to know if they'd reached Afghanistan.

Another thirty minutes or so in the air, and Bolan felt them dipping once more for a landing. Touchdown, taxi, park.

Not a sound beyond the circle of steel.

Then Bolan heard the first round of chugging, his gut twisting with tension, fingers clawing like talons. There was a faint cry of pain, a distant voice raised in angry disbelief, the muted chugging of sound-suppressed weapons pumping lead. A crash, a thud of deadweight, the floorboard vibrating beneath Bolan. There was silence, then he picked up the slightest vibration underfoot as someone closed on his steel circle.

"Belasko."

Bolan made out Poe's voice right on top of him. Now that they were grounded, no chance of depressurized sudden death, the Executioner was poised to make his launch, go for broke.

"I am going to open the door, Belasko. I am going to step back. Charge us, you will be shot where you stand."

He waited, his heartbeat throbbing in his ears, then the door snicked open. The Executioner unfolded, stiff again from being hemmed in the steel womb, but adrenaline oiled his limbs in a hurry as he stepped out of the cylinder.

And found the four-man control unit strewed down the cabin, pools of crimson spreading away from the tattered heaps locked in death.

The Executioner watched as Poe, the Beretta held low by his side, took a few more steps back, slipped the remote in his pants pocket.

"There's been a change in plans," Poe said. "But it was always in the works. The others have gone off to deal with the Hellboxes."

Bolan looked past Poe at the two hardmen, both of them wielding sound-suppressed Berettas.

"They're my men," Poe told Bolan. "The pilots. We're safe here for the moment. You and me need to have a talk."

Since first laying eyes on the man, it was the one time Bolan figured they could agree on something. Beyond the coming chat, though, the Executioner was all fire and steel to make his move to break out.

12

"That's the third time you've checked your watch in the last fifteen minutes, Mr. Decker. I would prefer you simply watch this miserable track of rock and dirt and let me worry about our cargo arriving on time."

From the back seat, Carlyle on his right, Jenkins wondered why their man in Afghanistan seemed overly concerned with his watch. A bump in the road, Jenkins banging his head off the jamb to spark his eyes with white light from a shooting pain across his scalp, and he silently cursed their chauffeur.

"Eyes on the road, Mr. Decker. Look at your watch again, and I will break it off your wrist and the hand to go with it."

The old man was pissed off but taking charge in a new tone that bordered fear.

The guy was clock-watching, but why? Jenkins wondered. The C-130, according to their control crew, was lagging behind by two hours and just over six hundred miles as it rumbled on at top speed, flying north at the moment over Pakistan, the airspace guaranteed for the Herc's safe passage by their ISI contact here, Colonel Mohammed Khandar. Again, the particulars escaped Jenkins, and time was a concept he gave up on once their flight halfway around the globe passed the thirty-six hour-mark. Roughly one-third of the journey had been spent on the ground, equal shares divided between a remote island in the Pacific, then once again on another tropical volcanic plug somewhere, he believed, in the Indian Ocean, if previous memory of flying over the diamond-glittering aqua sheet around the Maldive Islands served him right. Both times, ostensibly, they malingered on the ground to let the C-130 shave off some airspace. They refueled twice, the old man speaking over his handheld radio out of earshot for long stretches, expression unreadable.

And then there was the Belasko problem. At first, it galled him to believe the old man would actually bring the bastard onboard, part of the team. Never mind all the soldiers who'd been under his command sliced and diced by the badass. And what the hell was all that about, anyway? No hard feelings, the old man admired his talent, ready to sign the guy up, blank check, bonus and all. But it eventually became clear the old man was playing some kind of head game with Belasko, no intention of handing the man back his weapons, which were still stowed, nonetheless, in a compartment aboard their jet.

And still another hanging question. Why had the old man relented to Poe, allowed the man to just pick up and move the jets to a valley fifty, sixty miles east? Sure, the claim Poe made about possible treachery by the Taliban—who could ever tell about those guys anyway—raiding the jet to hold it until the deal was concluded to their satisfaction, sounded persuasive enough, if he thought it through. Still...

The world was suddenly feeling out of tilt to Jenkins. Whatever the game, he was growing tired of it. The unknown waited, and he saw it unfold as they cleared a rise. The headlights of their military-type jeep washed over a sprawling maze of stone dwellings, crumbled ruins of countless other structures like gravestones testifying to the ravages of the mujahadeen's ferocious stand against the Soviets. The camp, he heard the old man suddenly tell them, was on the other side—the northern outskirts—of the mountain village called Madjik. Jenkins looked forward into the side glass, caught the reflection of the lights of their caravan. Three jeeploads of his Z-Core, twelve guns in all, who'd flown in the other jet, another seventeen guns on the Hercules coming in soon to watch their backs. The canvas-draped troop carrier was last in line, the number of Taliban rebels in the rig equal to his own force, he knew. And all of them kept the AKMs and AK-47s close to their bodies, the only one of them who spoke English, Daoud, Jenkins recalled, having looked at the old man and then the rest of the Americans when they'd stepped off the jets as if he'd just blundered into camel dung.

Jenkins noted the armed shadows skulking around in the rubble as Decker led the caravan into Madjik. The warheads of a few bobbing RPG-7s poked out of the darker bowels where blue firelight burned from scattered fires. He couldn't see their eyes, but he could sense the hatred and distrust reaching out like some living burning fire. Jenkins felt his hands tighten their grip around his HK MP-5, damn grateful, too, the pockets of his windbreaker were stuffed with grenades, just in case it got real ugly.

Welcome to Afghanistan, he thought.

"I COPY."

Bolan listened, his body a coiled spring, the warrior braced to launch himself at the shadow man as one of the pilots let the handheld radio fall away from his face and told Poe, "Our people on the other bird have the nest clear of hostiles, sir. Situation under control."

Poe might have been in a talking mood, but the Beretta never wavered from a point aimed at Bolan's chest. "It's set to hit the fan, Belasko, or whatever your name really is. I need your help, but I always did."

"Meaning what exactly?"

"Meaning—"

"Since we're in this getting-to-know-you frame, how about getting those guns holstered."

"Fair enough." Poe and pilots stowed the Berettas in shoulder rigging. "Hey, if I'd wanted you dead, I could have simply dropped a few cyanide pellets down the chute. Are we clear I want to keep you alive?"

"We're not clear on a damn thing."

"Look, we've got a few minutes still. Why don't you grab a seat—"

"I'm tired of sitting."

"Okay, here it is. This is a black operation, a surgical strike my people have had on the drawing board for quite some time. It's true that we monitor black projects. The ones that go awry, translation some guy like the old man going for himself..."

"This Raven character?"

"Yeah, the old man."

"What's his real name?"

"Forget about it, it doesn't matter. Him, Jenkins, a bunch of other rat bastards we're about to flush out of the dark and stomp, here and back home—that matters. I've had my own operatives inserted under their noses almost since day one. I've had one man in this country almost since the day the Russians packed up and went home. Call him a friend of the mujahadeen. He's riding with the rats as we speak."

"And Rockwell?" Bolan asked, detecting no visible reaction one way or the other from Poe.

"He jumped ship."

"He also tried to put a bullet in the back of my head. One of your fine 'operative' types."

"I had smelled him out."

"Used me, you mean to say, to take care of a personal hemorrhoid."

"I had no choice."

"There's always a choice," Bolan growled. "You could have been straight with me from the start."

"Hey, you came to me, pal. You're here, the sky's getting ready to fall, and whether you like it or not, I may be the only help you have in getting out of this country in one piece when the smoke clears."

"Skip the friendly preamble. Bottom line."

"The old man's been around for a long, long time. He's some two-time war hero, medals out the wazoo. I've seen former presidents pour him a glass of whiskey like they were giddy barmaids graced with the presence of some Hollywood celebrity. I've had guys running around for years, damn near bowing in his presence, from Cheyenne Mountain back to Langley and all the way to sixteen-hundred P Ave. He couldn't cut it in civilian life. Three failed marriages, went belly up when he tried his hand in the restaurant business, some mom-and-pop Italian joint. Word was he liked his whiskey and veal parm and three sets of books in the back office more than... Anyway, he got back in the game. Connections. Respect. The intelligence world is run similar to the Mafia, the old school kind, that is, where a man makes his bones, shoots his way up the ranks. He became a power player, in spook terms on the fat end of the feeding chain, or a floater, to a common peasant like the late Mr. Rockwell. At first Opus Damocles was meant to be a counteroffensive program."

"The invasion scenario—the Russians, or now the Chinese, are coming. I heard it already."

"There's more. Nuclear waste and other fissionable matériel has been surging out of Los Alamos like a burst dam. The old man again working with some shadows in FEMA who seem to pray at the altar of his past glory. But the stink of the corruption goes all the way back to the Pentagon. A few key people have a plan, already in motion, to accomplish two goals. One—take out the traitors here, up-close and personal, confirmation the old man and his wild bunch are terminated. That's my job. Two—we've been searching for inroads to get our hands on Bin Laden, the Iranian and a shit load of terrorists who can escape Western justice while setting up shop here and keep the terror machine rolling. We're talking a massive terrorist launching point right here in this neighborhood. Sudanese. Lebanese. Syrians. Iranians. Iraqis. Taliban goons who are on the verge of taking over this country entirely, and if they do that, American interests are all but guaranteed to get kicked out the window in this part of the world. This camp also doubles as a warehouse transshipment point for most of the raw opium that goes over the mountains to Pakistan for refinement into heroin. Their C-130 is about thirty minutes, I'm told, from hitting Afghan airspace. It is going to happen virtually overtop this point where I'm trying to convince you I have your best interests in staying alive at heart."

"That's a definite reach from where I stand."

"Well, reach this. En route from a classified U.S. military base in Saudi, a flying armada—count ten B-2 Stealths, one B-52 loaded with conventional and non-nuclear payloads, one AC-130 Spectre gunship, tack on a fighting escort of F-15Es... You see where I'm headed with this?"

Bolan did, but that didn't solve his Poe problem.

"I see you. Wondering whether you can trust me. I don't blame you, but you have no choice. Here's the situation. Our guys will intercept that C-130 and blow it right out of the sky. It will happen in a prescoped area, courtesy of an SR-71 and the usual eyes in the sky, that is relatively uninhabited. Some Afghan shepherds or poppy pickers might fall ill a few months from now, cancer and such, but my report tells me the wind is blowing from the north, so we should be spared a radioactive dusting if we get out of Dodge in a few hours."

Say Poe was even handing off a partial truth. Bolan could read the writing on the wall if the guy was being straight. Afghanistan was the devil's cauldron of terrorist recruitment, training, a hiding hole for the wealthier fanatics, their launch point for past and planned future slaughter against the West. It was true enough they came from all over the Middle East and North Africa to hold hands in a show of jihad unity, the Taliban embracing their fellow warriors against the Great Satan. One big fundamentalist party where they thumbed their noses at Western law and intelligence agencies, could burrow themselves so deep in mountain strongholds it would take perhaps a hundred kilotons of nuclear rage to make sure they didn't crawl out of their nesting place to murder again. All right, Bolan knew the surgical strike Poe had claimed was knocking on the door would be buried so deep not even a blinding light would find it in the hallowed rings of the Pentagon. No media, no CNN. Not even Stony Man Farm, with all its hyper-tech and super-sleuthing through cyberspace, would catch the green light to bomb this part of Afghanistan into a smoking crater until after the fact. If some hacker or news type did, in fact, smell out the blood and hear the thunder, went public, blanket denials would be hurled all around.

It happened. Bolan had been there before.

"Where does it go from here?" the Executioner wanted to know.

"We fly back to where I waved bye-bye to the old man. One Jeep was left behind. I made a few reasonable demands, outbulled the bullshitter for a change. No Z-Core there. We ride in, the bombs fall. We move in, you and me, side by side. They'll be staggering around, if they survive the strafing from hell. March into the smoke and fire. Confirm, if there are any pieces left, the kills." Poe pointed to an overhead compartment. "Your gear and weapons, everything down to your satlink, are right there."

Bolan looked at Poe for a long moment. "So, my ending up here, it was just some quirk of fate."

"That's one way of putting it."

"Is there another?"

"I don't know, pal. Things happen. The cosmos works in mysterious ways, what can I tell you?"

"How about the truth?"

"I've handed it over to you. I don't expect you to swallow it hook, line and sinker, but when the fireworks start you might become a believer."

Bolan felt the cynical twist screwing up one side of his mouth. "You're one of the good guys, is that it?"

"That, and we're a long way from the finish line."

"Mr. Clean."

"White hat and all."

Bolan moved ahead, one eye on Poe and company, reached the compartment and pulled the latch. His options limited to zero, the Executioner was going to run with the program. Before the thought took shape in his mind, Poe spoke.

"I know. I so much as twitch a gun your way, it looks like I'm just a bullshit artist, feel free to put one between my eyes."

Bolan didn't say anything. It took him a full two minutes to check his weapons, the clips all around, lock and load, then finally snug the combat harness in place, enough grenades fixed and hanging, he figured, to educate and raze an entire village of terrorists. He appreciated the fact Mr. Poe had seen fit to let him keep the

hardware he'd taken from the gunners in New Mexico.
All beefed up and somewhere to go.

The Executioner looked Poe dead in the eye and told
him, "I will."

13

What little he knew about Afghanistan had come to Jenkins following a monologue from the old man during layover number two. Item—a fourteen-year stretch of killing and mayhem, ending about four years after the Soviet evacuation, and the old man pinned a conservative figure of a million Afghans dead from war and starvation during that period. Item—five million folks fleeing the battle-scarred country and memories of hell on Earth, as civil war broke out between rival tribes bent on inventing their own vision of tomorrow, and Pakistan and Iran became open refugee quagmires where another million or so starved or crawled to the grave from disease. Item—either war or simple deforestation had nearly stripped the country to a barren moonscape, the only forests left high up in the mountains, where trees were chopped down by rebel bands at a rate that would have alarmed environmentalists worldwide, that was assuming they could have stopped wringing their hands and fretting about some whales and the Amazon jungle basin long enough to bother looking toward the Hindu Kush to hoist a new banner for the sake of the ozone or Mother Nature. These new and heavily armed entrepreneurs trucked the firewood to the most desperate of poor villages where there was no electricity—gasoline and kerosene a luxury reserved for those wielding the power of money or the gun—those tribes often trading in most of their hardware to rebels in exchange for a mere week's supply of heat. Bullets weren't much use when a person was freezing to death and didn't have wood to build a fire to cook the kebab. Not much by way of farmland, either, since the Soviets had seen fit to concentrate on mining huge tracts of fertile soil with such an intricate network of booby traps—more than a few of which were laced with nerve gas—and some shepherd's son was still losing an arm or a leg to this very day.

Just what he needed to hear, Jenkins had thought then, stats and stories, when all of them were flying into the unknown, putting it all on the line, and for what? Dead was dead, and it didn't matter if he had ten million or ten billion to his name. But the old man had to have read the weary concern and forged on to spite him, just the same. So farming had become the number-one hazardous occupation, but, of course, opium was the cash crop of Afghanistan, the bulk of which was jealously harvested, guarded and shipped over the mountains by various warrior clans. A billion plus a year, again a conservative figure, for drugs sold to the Pakistanis and Iranians, for still more guns falling into the hands of drug-running rebels who were building up their army by the day to storm the gates of Kabul, take down the palace and insert themselves as the people's saviors.

Jenkins had wondered back then what the point of the info sound bite was all about, the old man reciting the basics, but nothing solid handed off about their next course on the other end or, more precisely, his own role clearly mapped out.

Then it hit Jenkins, a bolt of lightning, as they crossed a stretch of no-man's borderland between the village ruins and the camp, and he took a closer look into the watching eyes of the armed shadows. As a former mercenary, he was long since hardened to the suffering of natives in a foreign backwater—the unwashed he always determined he would just as soon shoot as look at if they gave him any crap whatsoever. But there was a message coming clear from the old man's history lesson, the words somehow suddenly taking on living shape before his eyes, a warning bell clanging in his skull, putting him on the edge of his seat when their jeep cleared the last block of rubble and ventured deeper into the armed camp.

The numerous campfires were staggered around the sprawling banks of tents, gaps here and there showing the dark bulk of military vehicles. A blue sheen illuminated the way for their caravan, seemed to guide them like some beacon from hell toward whole waiting armies of Taliban guerrillas, not to mention the gaggles of foreign terrorists of every shade and questionable intent eyeballing their entrance. Jenkins saw more AK-47s and RPGs, more turbans and menacing scowls framed in those scraggly bird's-nest beards made famous by Western media snippets on Bin Laden's Afghan vacation roost than he could have dreamed up in his worst and wildest soldier-of-fortune AFU scenario.

Now he understood the finer points of the old man's lecture, or believed he did as a fresh wave of anxiety froze him to his seat. War, deprivation and suffering were simply a way of life here. Not too unlike his African forays—where a white merc was treated by the natives with some degree of respect, especially if some cash was on hand or a ready bottle of whiskey could be offered like the old Indian peace pipe—but one look at the countless pairs of dark eyes staring their way and he knew these men didn't give a damn if they lived or died. Their eyes told Jenkins the whole grim story. The new arrivals were the enemy, nothing more, nothing less. Fresh infidel meat, he deduced, that could well get skinned and skewered, maybe just to pass some idle time.

Decker put on the brakes, Jenkins watching as the transport truck pulled alongside and Daoud leaned out the window. "Follow us."

And they did. Camels and donkeys meandered the campsite, a lone sheep traipsing past Jenkins's search of the blue light. They stopped near the largest tent, Jenkins falling out, SMG slung around his shoulder.

"This way," Daoud said.

From across the front of their jeep, the old man told Decker, "Stay outside with the others."

The stink of dung and the sweet tang of hash were so strong Jenkins thought the smell might bowl him off his feet, but fear and a burning desire to get this business wrapped up and on his way out of Afghanistan kept him marching on, the old man beside him. Daoud was smiling as he held back a thick wool blanket and beckoned with his AK-47 that they should keep moving.

Jenkins found himself crunching the old man's numbers as he squeezed past Daoud. A million dead here, a million there, sudden death just a simple matter of the day's progression, something expected, routine, like sitting down for dinner. The former soldier of fortune suddenly wondered if all of them were going to end up just another statistic, only they'd stack up a body count that wouldn't see any mortician's ledger. Jenkins figured the buzzards in Afghanistan were the only ones who ate on a regular basis.

"FIREBIRD ONE to Night Jackal, come in, Night Jackal."

The flight to the waiting jeep went off without a hitch. The M-16 cradled in his hands, and with one 40 mm round up the snout of the M-203, Bolan gave Poe a look as the handheld radio crackled on the shadow man's belt. His expression had to have said it all, because Poe grunted, a twist to the thin slash of his mouth. "Like my handle, do you? If the shoe fits..."

Bolan gave the rugged landscape a roving search. Clear skies, swathed in starlight, a half-moon. The sawtooth peaks of formidable mountains ringed the narrow valley where the jets had touched down. While Poe took the call, Bolan dumped his war bag in the back seat of a jeep that had seen better days. The black paint job was scarred across the hood, likewise Bolan's door, from where bullets had left their angry calling card. Two dents where the driver had slammed into something or someone on the panel just behind the passenger door, a near matching indentation on the engine housing just above the left front wheel.

"Night Jackal here."

"Spectre's in position, Night Jackal, going in for the

kill. The boom will lower, two minutes and counting, then it's all systems go on Tango Base."

"Roger that, Firebird One. Stay in touch. Out."

Bolan took the passenger seat as Poe climbed in behind the wheel. A Colt Commando assault rifle was the shadow man's choice for main weapon, pistol holstered, Poe already having snugged on the combat harness and fixed the grenades and clips during the brief return trip. Whatever Poe's angle, Bolan knew he had no choice but to take this ride to the end of the line. Sometimes it happened like that, and Bolan knew the deal, at least on his side of the fence. His back was to the wall, trust no one, come out swinging. From where he stood, if it was armed it was fair game.

Poe checked his watch, in no hurry to get the jeep moving. "Just in case you have some doubts about what I told you, let's sit tight for a minute. I parked it myself when the old man left, angled so you could catch the opening act. Why don't we listen to the sound of silence, enjoy it while it lasts."

"I AM CALLED Ghazni."

Jenkins looked at the five mullahs, holy men or whatever they were supposed to be, sitting Indian-style on colored pillows. Dark eyes bored through him and the old man, reading into their looks, and Jenkins wondered if he was supposed to bow and kiss their hands. The white-bearded, black-turbaned Ghazni assumed the middle spot, flanked by his holy men, and Jenkins was struck by a sense of déjà vu as he found himself standing in the shadows, kerosene light flickering over their faces. Minus the high-tech trimmings, the mullahs had their poor man's version of the Room.

The old man got down to business, a quick look around the tent having told Jenkins he might want to be ready for anything. "I understand the Iranian went into hiding in the mountains. I understand he's suddenly come down with a case of shaky nerves. I understand he may not have all of my money. I understand he's maybe thinking this is all some sort of elaborate design on my part to bag him and haul him back to the United States to stand trial for various, uh, business endeavors he's engaged in recently."

While the old man told the holy men how much he understood, Jenkins was scoping out their surroundings. Long tables planted here and there, heaped with bowls, half-eaten loaves of bread. Cast-iron stove in the far corner, kerosene lanterns hung from the tent poles. A quick head count and he tallied up twenty-two Taliban goons, twenty-seven if he factored in the holy turbans with their AK-47s laid in the dirt beside their pillows. He was looking at the mullahs when the radio crackled to life on the old man's belt. He didn't need the C-130's pilot squawking out the SOS, the man's frantic tone telling him in no uncertain terms it was going to hit the fan up there. Jenkins heard the pilot shouting that their radar screens were lighting up with unknowns, presumably hostiles, a big mother ship off to their starboard, the pilot rattling off the range and altitude of the flying battleship, a Spectre, before the copilot bellowed that the port windows of the gunship were opening up, guns sticking out.

"Holy mother of..."

He tuned out the pilot, the world around Jenkins freezing to some brittle mist of suspended white light. The pounding of his heart kept driving the blood pressure into his ears, the sudden cold fear he felt holding him partly blind for another long terrible moment.

"We're under fire!"

Jenkins heard them screaming, caught the old man's curse as the white sheet lifted in his eyes and he found the holy men glaring his way, murder in their eyes, clearly thinking their American visitors had come bearing gifts of treachery. Jenkins heard an explosion rumble over the airwaves, the pilots screaming in new raised levels of terror, static, then nothing but dead silence.

And then it turned ugly in the tent.

THE THUNDER ROLLED toward them from the south. It was a distant rumble, far beyond the wall of granite. It seemed to drop straight down from the heavens themselves, but Bolan managed to catch the sky lighting up in that direction, a wink of firelight at first, then some glowing band held, expanding in brilliant shades of white, yellow, orange and red across the sky. Firebird One called and informed Night Jackal phase one of Mission Devil's Mercy was successfully concluded. Poe cranked on the engine, lurched the jeep ahead. "I have a spot scoped out by my man on the ground here. Due southeast of the camp. Some speed and a little luck, and we'll make it just in time to catch the show."

"Your man on the ground know he's about to get toasted?"

"He accepted that fact going in, although he'll attempt to shoot his way out or through anyone who gets in his way. The bombing, maybe three-fourths of it, will be confined to the immediate campsite. The village of Madjik is pretty much a place where we won't find too many family oriented types. Still, there will be some civilian casualties."

Bolan felt the ball in his gut, sickened for a moment at the thought that even a few women and children were slated for slaughter. Innocents getting cut down in the cross fire was a fact of war, he knew, but that didn't mean he had to accept it. The person at the top, calling the shots on this surgical strike to remove the cancer of international terrorism here, obviously didn't care who got killed as long the end result was achieved. Again, Bolan didn't have to plunge himself into a dark hole of questionable morality concerning the needless, indiscriminate taking of the life of a child or a mother just to hear himself say "mission accomplished." A warrior could do battle against the enemy, slay them in the most gruesome and vicious ways imaginable, he knew, and still retain his humanity where the noncombatants were concerned.

The jeep was barreling ahead, full speed, practically flying over the ruts in the broken but arrow-straight track of ground, when the Executioner made out the distant but familiar scream of turbofan engines from the south. The sky was minutes away from falling, Bolan knew, the gaping jaws of death opening wide on the other end, ready to greet or swallow him and his flaky sidekick with all the insatiable hunger only death knew.

14

Nothing short of a miracle would save him from the conflagration on the way. Living on stolen time, wriggling out of tight jams like a human eel wasn't something new to him, but the Company's special op in Afghanistan would most certainly count his blessings if he cleared ground zero with nothing other than dings, gashes and a ringing bell. At worst, some third-degree burns if the firestorm reached out to fry a little of his grizzled bacon, and if the pain was too intense there was morphine stashed in a small hovel he'd staked out as his home on the southern edge of the village. Assuming he even lived long enough to feel the pain. Assuming, also, the place was still standing after the sky fell.

He was an old soldier at this kind of dirty deal, where the opposition was led to believe he was playing ball, a straight shooter working a sweet transaction for contraband on their behalf while he pulled the strings from the shadows, helping to oil the machine of their destruction. He'd known Raven since the days when they'd trained the shah's secret police, SAVAK, and made some inroads to the Taliban's latest guest on the terror scene there in Afghanistan. Man, that was a long time ago, he thought, taking the money from a wet-behind-the-ears rich kid who would go on to become one of the world's most wanted terrorists. Actually protecting the guy when the Ayatollah and his mullahs wanted to pilfer the kid's inheritance. Getting the kid safely relocated to Beirut where he'd gone on to bigger and better things.

A treacherous journey, no doubt, the powers-that-be on his side talking out of both sides of their mouths, straddling the fence, working both sides. Good guys, bad guys, who the hell could tell anymore? One day a fundamentalist was their best friend, helping to further American interests. Tomorrow the same guy was on their shit list. Go figure. Years of wading in the cesspool of his side's deceit and "special interests." All the cutthroats and backstabbers lurking in every shadow, guys on both sides going for themselves while he maneuvered all the pieces into place to help their corner of the world blow up in their faces.

Such was the case here, only tonight this stretch of real estate would get far more than just a taste of hell. And he had already made his decision to put his life at the threshold of extinction to get all the players assembled on the field.

Well, almost all of them, at any rate.

A final check of his watch, and he broke into the first few casual steps of that stroll he pictured in his mind on the ride in. Stay cool, that was the key. Maybe tell them he had to take a leak, if one of them was inclined to question the sudden foray into the darkness. It was a stroke of luck, at the very least, that Raven had left him outside with the shooters. If he'd been ordered inside the tent, there was no chance he could cut and run, not with Dauod and the wall of Taliban goons guarding the powwow, a staggered line of fundamentalists reaching all the way from the entrance to the meet inside, staggered down the sides of their motor pool.

The HK MP-5 around his shoulder was some reassurance he could nail the first few human hurdles before he broke into his mad sprint, but his hands were already delving into the pockets of his windbreaker, wrapping around the cold steel of the frag grenades. He would need some distraction, envisioned dropping a moment of shock and panic into the pack of shadows around the jeeps. The plan looked solid enough, at least in his mental picture of the mayhem he intended to wreak.

Reality had a way of obliterating scripted images, though, when the chaos and confusion of real-time battle erupted. It would all come down to a few critical heartbeats if he was going to pull it off.

A part of him still couldn't believe it had even gotten this far.

A Company operative in Saudi had briefed him on his secured satlink less than a day ago. And he gave Decker the critical list of particulars, right down to the minute when the flying fury would unload Armageddon on this sprawling haven for more than two hundred terrorists. If there were any flaws in the concept of a surgical air strike, he couldn't find them. The problem wasn't what the flying armada would or wouldn't do. The flyboys had the advantage of shock, not to mention speed and altitude all to themselves. And by the time most of the place was cleared out from the first strafing, the Stingers he'd helped get into the country back when the Company chose the mujahadeen as the lesser of two evils during the Russian invasion... Well, it took a little time to crank up the Stingers, and he'd seen the rebels weren't all that adept with something any more complicated than an AK-47. The ones he had trained personally and who had become somewhat proficient with the Stingers were long since dead. War. The elements. Starvation. There was death enough all over the country to go around. Just because, he thought, CNN wasn't over in this neck of the woods tromping around didn't mean they weren't killing one another by the droves on an hourly basis from the Khyber Pass to Kabul.

No, the glitches were turning up on the ground, the nature of the beasts he dealt with on a daily basis rearing suspicious and paranoid heads from their rat's burrows. Bin Laden had suddenly disappeared. The Iranian, heir to the Kahmujouti billions, had also vacated the premises, presumably hiding out in the mountains to the east, perhaps instinct sniffing out some ill wind blowing his way. And the drug-dealing Pakistani scumbag and ISI company were likewise conveniently nowhere to be found. He knew the ISI contact had been in touch with Raven, the old man touching base with Khandar over a field radio as soon as he'd stepped off the jet. He knew Khandar had his own little command post somewhere in a village to the far west. The idea— or so the man said—was for the Pakistanis to monitor the situation from a distance, watch the backs of their American counterparts. Another problem surfaced in his thoughts. Khandar had a portable radar unit. It stood to reason the flying armada were jamming the works from their end, but still...

"Hey, Decker! Where the hell you going?"

His heart lurching, Decker slowed, pulled out the

first steel egg, pulled the pin. No sooner was he hurling the first frag bomb at the old man's shooters than number two was armed and flying at the Taliban sentries. With any luck they'd start shooting up one another, every man for himself, both sides thinking they had been duped. Enough breathing room, he hoped, to start him running for his life.

DESPERATION EXUDED its own stink, which, he determined, was closely related to its cousin, fear. Jenkins found his nose cloyed by a smell that told him the truth of the moment, and nothing but.

It was over. They were finished. The two cousins, fear and desperation, he saw, were etched on the old man's face like some gravestone. The only thing missing was their names. If he hadn't seen it himself, he would have thought it impossible. The man with all the answers—all of which he had kept to himself all along—looked hopelessly lost. Damn near childlike, on the verge of a hissy fit because he wasn't going to get what he demanded.

"What is the meaning of this, American? Explain yourself this instant!"

The holy man was rising, smooth, boneless, like a wisp of smoke, when it happened. Jenkins couldn't say for sure what set the old man off exactly, but the ex-merc had no choice but to go for it in the next eye blink. Especially after the twin thunderclaps of grenades—one blast going off right on the heels of the other—sounded beyond the tent. And who the hell was out there anyway, blowing guys up, maybe wasting their ride out of there in the process? Was it that conveniently MIA Pakistani contact? Maybe caught the word somehow his comrade in the ISI had been eighty-sixed and now he was looking to return the favor?

It didn't matter, Jenkins decided, since it became evident he might never have to worry about a taxi ride back to the jets, anyway.

Jenkins armed his grenade, lobbed it off to his left into a pack of holy men who were watching the shredded remains of something red and wet blowing inside the tent on a boiling cloud of cordite and dust. The old man was already drilling bullets into the enemy, his pistol barking like there was no tomorrow. Jenkins figured it was something like two, maybe three hundred to one odds against the visitors, that they were nags destined to wind up buzzard meat.

The grenade erupted, scything steel hornets through the enemy ranks. Jenkins figured he was finished anyway, so why not take out as many turbans as he could before the bullets started ripping into him? A voice, though, in the back of his churning thoughts, clung to hope, told him there was the slimmest chance he could make it outside the tent if he fired on the run and charged the canvas beyond the falling red tatters of holy men. The old man was angling off the other way, drilling two, maybe three neat red holes through turbans before the enemy got their act together and lined him up with their AK-47s.

Jenkins was sweeping the subgun around, hosing a few rebels, surging ahead, when the first of several explosions seemed to vaporize the tent to his rear. The next thing Jenkins knew he was sailing, the world lit up all around in blinding light.

IT WAS QUITE the spectacle.

And they were taking the mother of all shellackings down there.

Even at a guesstimate of five hundred yards, give or take, Bolan claimed a ringside seat. The marching lines of explosions, the six F-15-Es screaming past the climbing inferno and soaring to the north—there was a hellish combo of such sense-cleaving noise, Bolan might as well have been right on top of the action.

Their own kill nest was a few yards up the incline from their vehicle. The curtain had gone up just when Poe had cut to the east from the crumbled wall at the southern edge of the village. The first high-tech spears of doom were streaking toward the camp on flaming tails.

Madjik, the soldier thought, settling in a dip behind a low wall of broken rock. Any magic at that moment was shown off by American fighter pilots. The show of destruction had only just begun.

Grim, Bolan watched, listened to the rolling thunder. Laser-guided missiles had slammed into selected targets and gone off in their raging mushroom balls of fire, hurling stick figures and what was left of other mangled rebel vultures into the air by the dozens. A good number of vehicles were blown into scrap, two clustered motor pools needing no more than a single hit, fuel igniting in ruptured tanks to further fan the inferno.

The Executioner had the M-16 set on the ground, an easy grab, but he decided to field-test the new HK sniper rifle, burn up some of his late enemy's ammo and hold off expending his supply for as long as possible. The soldier lifted the piece. It felt smooth, light in his hands, both, he figured, by its design and the adrenaline firing his blood.

No matter how much death from above hammered the camp, Bolan knew there would be survivors. One hundred percent casualties, even from a saturation bombing of the smart variety, could never be guaranteed, unless, of course, that B-52 dropped a gravity nuke from its belly.

The Executioner waited, spotted the first of several enemy runners headed his way. A rolling wave of screaming turbofans hit him from some point high in the heavens, and the Executioner looked up to find the batlike shapes of the Stealth bombers soaring in to unload the next round.

Bolan would hold out for another minute, two tops, while Act Two commanded center stage. He would allow the rabbits to shave some distance to his death sights, then he'd join the hunt.

THE BIGGER QUESTIONS would never get answered now, but the why of it all was no longer a pressing issue for Jenkins.

Survival would prove an ordeal all by itself.

Somehow he'd been thrown clear of the hell eating up the camp and the village for as far as he could see beyond the fuzz in his eyes. Grounded at some point beyond the tent, engulfed in flames, looking down from some incline, Jenkins wondered if he was being guided by some divine intervention. How else could he explain not getting blown to bloody bits? Those were fighter jets, smart bombs and such, wasting whole gaggles of terrorists, lighting up their heat-seeking screens, most likely, easy pickings, pilots locked on, a touch of the gun sticks. Hard to say at first what the flying demons were, since he was straining to hear the roar of turbofans beyond the ringing in his ears. Americans? Or the Pakistanis? He didn't think it was the Pakistani air force. Too close to home for the Pakistanis to risk the wrath of nervous neighbors with this kind of Armageddon. Some U.S. black operation, then, the old man's auction of the Hellboxes to an Iranian fanatic rooted out at the last minute by some godlike power in the American military infrastructure. He couldn't say, would probably never know.

And what did it matter, anyway?

They were screaming in midflight, flying shadows riding the tidal walls of fire. He rolled onto his back, listened to the cries of men dying all over the camp, all manner of garbage plunking to earth to either side, a coppery odor in his nose, pinching like ammonia-dipped fingers but helping to clear out some of the cobwebs just the same. Bat-shaped creatures came into view, high in the sky, way up there, it seemed, skimming beneath the stars.

Stealth bombers.

Jenkins heard the grim chuckle cracking through the ringing and the throbbing in his ears. The old man had walked all of them into some covert U.S. bombing raid. The stickers had been stuck.

What was that? he thought, as he felt his hand slap down on something solid, metallic. The pain shot like a butcher's knife hacking at his neck as he twisted his head. And found, thank God, the HK MP-5 had flown along beside him.

No point in malingering.

Jenkins spit the blood from his mouth, touched a

sticky gash that had split his scalp to the bone and somehow found the strength to stand. A look back, and he saw the flying devil bats were dropping the works on the village proper. Nothing came out of the firewall savaging the tent of the holy men. Nothing except the nauseating stench of roasting flesh.

Time to go.

But where? And do what?

One gun against how many? There were sure to be survivors, Taliban goons and whoever else looking to vent some serious hate and rage on any Western type wandering around.

Whatever, this game was dead. And so was the old man. Everyone was on his own, no exceptions.

Jenkins decided to leg it out of there, head for the hills to the east. He was turning away from the ocean of fire when he spied a shadow rise from the ground. It was the briefest glimpse, Jenkins wondering if the firelight was casting some ghostly illusion, when the flaming finger opened up, rising from the earth as if the tracking fire had a mind of its own. He felt the bullets tearing into his back at a fiery point just beneath his ribs.

15

The Spectre was third in the lineup, which meant, Bolan figured, the B-52 was on deck, hitting cleanup. He could be wrong, but Executioner couldn't imagine there was much left standing for the Stratofortress when it stepped up to the plate.

The bat-configured shadows that were the Stealths hit the skies beyond the climbing mountain of fire in a silent staggered formation, up, up and away, gone, swallowed by the heavens after dumping their payload.

The AC-130 gunship went to work as soon as the last of the gravity bombs had gone off in the heart of the village, a behemoth dark battleship skirting along maybe five hundred feet above and just west of the soldier's vantage point.

Damn near on top of him. The nap-of-the-earth run told Bolan the crew didn't seemed overly concerned with risking the ire of some turbaned Rambo who might take it with a lucky shot from, say, a Stinger, or maybe there was an antiaircraft battery, but discerning much more than a few runners headed his way was out of the question for the soldier. The spectre, he figured, had the playing field all to itself. Anyone fool enough to crawl out of the smoke and fire to attempt a surface-to-air counterattack...well, Bolan suspected any survivors down there were likely more concerned about burrowing a deeper hole and riding it out, imploring God to deliver them than they were with hoisting a rocket and going for what was a long shot anyway. The entire camp, he saw, and at least three-quarters of the village were lit up, one sprawling funeral pyre.

Bolan's senses were shattered again as Spectre's portside artillery opened up with its gods of thunder. The warrior was well-acquainted with the massive firepower of the giant flying killer, had seen it in action during previous campaigns when he'd used it to soften up a target before wading into the killing ground to mop up.

The Executioner cradled the sniper piece, a 50-round magazine in place. No point in getting caught dry on the killing touch when there were still enemy heads aplenty. No need for thermal imaging, either, since the firestorm was framing faces in living color in the thin black crosshairs as he adjusted the scope and brought the first enemy gunner into view.

Locked on, good to go.

The Taliban goon was scrambling to his feet, shouting over his shoulder when Bolan squeezed the trigger. A brief eyeful of the gunner flying away from a red halo, and Bolan swung his aim, caught the shock and horror of Number Two Taliban reacting to the sight of his comrade getting waxed at near arm's length, and Bolan cored a .308 round into his face just above his hawkish nose.

He lowered the rifle and spotted more shadows popping up from the broken ground beyond the inferno of their camp, breaking into a hard charge for what they believed would be the safety of the foothills.

The only freedom guaranteed from there on, he knew, would come by way of death liberating the inner man.

"Looks like a plan, Belasko. Nice work."

Bolan turned and found Poe grinning toward the carnage, field glasses coming away from his eyes, the firelight wavering over the shadow man's face, showing the soldier a startling portrait of a death's head.

Poe slipped his nylon satchel across his shoulder after he filled his hand with the HK-69 grenade launcher, then wedged it inside a strap of his webbing. Bolan grunted, a mean grin cutting one corner of his mouth. "Yeah, I noticed you helped yourself."

The ghoul's grin held. "Nothing gets by you, but I'd be disappointed otherwise." Even though they were nearly on top of each other, they were forced to shout as the Spectre's bombardment thundered on. "Hey, you liberated it from a dead man, anyway. Besides, you've got plenty of edge already. Here it is, Chief. I'm going down. You cover my back for a few minutes while I make my way in?"

"And then what?"

"Well, I'll move from the north, counterclockwise through whatever's left standing after the B-52 makes it run. I need confirmation, and I have a good idea of where to start." He showed Bolan a small box with a digital screen. "Mother's little helper here, and I can coordinate the air strike. This puppy's even got GPS. I've got pre mapped grids and quads down to the yard tying me in to the flight crews. The wonders of high-tech. I can have those flyboys homed in on an insect picking at a severed arm, if I want to. Suggestion. Once I make it to the northern edge, I might need your assistance. Try and parallel me, keep a mental gauge best you can of my position, stick to roughly a hundred yards, if possible, in case I call in a few F-15s or the bats."

Bolan heard his mental radar for trouble blipping off the screen. What was to stop Poe from calling in the flying killing machines and blowing him off the face of Afghanistan?

"I see you're Mr. Suspicious. You can stay here, if you want. I may or may not make it back. If I don't, you're on your own."

"I'm already on my own."

"Whatever, tough guy."

"Get moving," Bolan told Poe. "I'll fall in behind you shortly."

Poe nodded, hefted the Colt Commando assault rifle and ventured the first few steps down the rocky incline. The Spectre, Bolan saw, was clearing out, rumbling on, leaving in its wake new firestorms so vicious and potent in their eye-hurting dazzle, they reached out, intercoursing with other fireballs, whole village blocks up in roaring flames with infernos swirling in some cyclonic fury.

No time to spare for admiring the view of a holocaust. The Executioner dropped two more Taliban rabbits, then checked on Poe as he broke into a run heading north. Bolan thought he saw a muzzle-flash in the distance beyond the firewall eating up what remained of the sea of tents. A harder search, and he saw another shadow plunging to the ground. Grimly curious, the soldier decided it was worth a closer study as he peered through the scope, fine-tuning the focus. Something was definitely falling apart in that direction, and since he lived in hope he was looking for the added bonus that maybe the savages were now eating one another.

"You shot me."

"So I did."

The voice drifted over him, calm, like the horror show raging beyond them was no big deal.

As if to say, "So what's the problem?"

Jenkins had dragged himself a few feet ahead on his elbows, going for his subgun, when he'd rolled his head around for some reason, uncertain of what he had seen. Or, more precisely, unable to believe the first glimpse of the face could possibly be the shooter in question. It couldn't be. No way, he thought. And after all he'd done, all the suffering...obedient and loyal.

Go figure, he thought. He was the dog now, reduced to a steaming pile about to get stepped in. Whoever said life was fair?

And he discovered it was all too terribly real, thinking the next life was just one long obscene joke, played on him, as he braced to face the ugly punch line.

The old man was stepping toward him, the AK-47 the weapon he'd used to cut him down from behind. For a moment, he found it incredible not only that the old man had escaped the initial holocaust of the bombing run, but that he'd walked into the meet armed only with a pistol, blown clear to produce an assault rifle to even any odds against lurking Taliban shooters.

Fate was, indeed, a fickle bitch.

The sky was roaring all around Jenkins, distorting sound, the blazing umbrella of firelight hurling dancing shadows in his eyes. He couldn't tell what was what, man or machine, shadows or moving objects, the whole spectrum of unreality meshing together in its sickening obscenity, tricking his senses, the churning puke in his belly a moment away from gushing forth. What he did know was that he couldn't feel his legs, instinct then horror telling him what that meant, the terrible swelling pressure in his gut warning him some vital organ had ruptured and he was filling up with blood, a human balloon about to burst at the seams.

Jenkins watched as the old man, his face streaked with crimson, stared back from the burning sky. It felt like an eternity before another round of hellacious rolling thunder finally ceased, and something that looked as big as a cruise ship floated overhead. More thunder split his skull, then gradually lessened to a sort of rumbling peal.

"Why?" It was all Jenkins could think to ask.

The old man gave a casual shrug, the muzzle of the AK-47 looking to Jenkins as if it were no more than a few inches from his face.

"It went to hell," the old man growled. "Just when I thought I was about to turn the corner, it all blew up in my face. Life works like that sometimes, sad to say. Those are American planes, son. Someone knew all along, thinking they had my number. Someone screwed me, I screw them back, only my package is proved bigger. The whole world just became my shooting gallery, son, my one last fat roll of Charmin. If it makes you feel any better, I wasn't going to keep you onboard the gravy train anyway, even if these towel heads had dealt straight."

"You used me."

"That was always part of the plan. I needed a few good men to pull this thing off. Some guys to watch my back, fair enough. Guys nobody cared about, nobody would miss if they bit the dust. Losers, like you. Getting the felons a walk wasn't easy. Hell, I had to hold a gun myself on one judge in Cleveland. Funny, though, about the persuasive power of money when all else fails."

"Is that..." Jenkins felt the white-hot pain knife through his side. "Money? All this was about the money?"

"That, and putting it all behind. Personal failure, that is. Failed business. A few bitchy, snippy ex-wives, never satisfied no matter what, voices, I tell you, that would make a man cry out for that nail over a chalkboard, that is if he wasn't shouting inside for a quick death. Kids don't care if you live or die as long as the wallet's open. What can I say? Guess civilian life and me weren't the match made in heaven I'd hoped for. So, from here, maybe grease a few wheels somewhere else, set up the Hellbox factory in, say, Lebanon, Sri Lanka maybe. Hell, they're looking for an edge all over the map these days. Relocation wouldn't be difficult at all. Not going to happen unless I cut and run. Sorry, I really am. All that's left is to clean up and bail."

"I looked at you...up to you...like..."

Jenkins choked on the words.

The old man snorted. "Like the father you never even laid eyes on. I know. I counted on your soft spot that way. If it makes you feel any better, I never saw my old man, either, after he left my mother. I was nine. Hate his guts to this day. I still hear that critical voice of his in my head. The usual. Never amount to anything. Always a disappointment, like it was my fault or something I was even born, stupid kid. God bless the guy. Guess all the torment helped motivate me in certain moments, get ahead, kick ass, find myself, make my own destiny. All I know is I made it in the world, left my mark. Of course, I can probably never go back to the States, but America's finished in the next ten years or so anyway. All it's going to take is one major economic collapse and the sheep will take to the streets. No gas. No money in the bank. No job. Never had much faith in human nature. People make me ill. Until I met you. Sounds strange, under the circumstances, I know. But I liked you. I really did."

Jenkins heard the bitter chuckle from his lips, a faraway hollow sound. "Glad I didn't disappoint...you rotten bastard."

"That's me. Colonel Bastard. Son, there are two kinds of men in this world. Those who take, and those who are taken from."

From the fog, Jenkins became gradually aware he'd found his subgun, mind registering, from the burning needles of pain, that his fingers were curling around the barrel, ready to haul it in, go for it even though the move would prove his last act of manhood. It didn't matter. The search was over. He was born to be nothing, and to nothing he would go.

A part of him couldn't wait to get there. Maybe the unknown held some peace. Maybe not. As far as anything mattered anymore, it was worth the gamble.

"We're not finished talking. I figure I owe you that much, son."

"You don't owe me jack shit."

"Oh, but I do. Freeze it there."

For some reason he did as he was told. He owed the strange obedience to some sense of twisted loyalty even then, when he knew the old man was seconds away from chopping him up with the AK-47. Leave him there for the buzzards. While he skipped off, probably boarded his jet and flew to whatever his next destination. Regroup. Jump-start the Hellbox program, try again. Even clinging to the last breath, he still wanted...what? Another chance? Acceptance? A fucking pat on the back?

"Son, I'll raise a glass of whiskey to your memory later."

And that was the last thing the old man said.

Jenkins made the decision to try to bring the subgun up and around, dish back some of the pain he felt, when the old man was kicked off his feet. He didn't hear the shot, but the way the old man toppled, feet swept out from under him, falling to his left, half of his skull, at least, erupting like rotten melon, Jenkins knew it was a distance shot. A sniper perched in the foothills. East.

Maybe Belasko? he wondered. If it was, it was all somehow fitting, he decided. Jenkins angled his body toward the mountains. He could imagine whoever had taken out the old man was right then lining up his grinning mug in crosshairs. No problem. Take the shot. It wasn't the way he'd ever pictured himself going out, something heroic like charging the bush where a dozen guerrillas were closing in or some Alamo-type last stand.

But this was his moment. Checking out, stiff upper lip. Fateful and final. At least he could take it like a man.

16

If Bolan could have read lips, magnified at eight-hundred-plus meters, he might have figured out the drama playing out in his scope. Then again, nothing about this Hellbox campaign surprised him anymore. He would never know why the old man had shot the man he knew as Jenkins. He would never know why it had all gone to hell with the Taliban in the first place. He couldn't even be certain the Hellboxes were destroyed, since his trust and faith in Poe to tell the truth were less than zero. And he suspected, given all the buzzards he'd encountered so far flapping off in their own directions, eating up who and whatever they could as they went—doing their own thing, whatever that was—that a couple of wanted international savages had already spread their wings and flown the coop. He couldn't say for certain, and at the moment it didn't matter.

A whole lot of killing was still on the menu.

Whatever the reason for the old man's latest round of treachery, Bolan dropped the curtain on that particular drama, the only worthy applause, the way he saw it.

All the criteria worked out to get the sniping job done, and Bolan tapped the trigger, the old man filling his scope for another heartbeat, then Bolan found his .308 round emptied at a spot just above the old man's earhole.

Blasted out of sight.

Bolan didn't malinger admiring the gruesome artwork, swinging the rifle right away to fill the scope with Jenkins.

And what was this all about? he wondered, as Bolan found Jenkins nearly staring him dead center in the crosshair, a portrait of torture that went way beyond mere physical pain. The guy looked like he wanted to have a talk, spill his guts about something, and if Bolan crouched there long enough the soldier would have also sworn something inside Jenkins was radiating, lighting up his face and rearranging his features. Impossible, of course, the target glowing, appearing ready to float out of there on wings of fire. Could have been the firelight obscuring real time. Could have been a whole flood of emotions jamming up the inner man. The word "profound," he thought, had been so mis- and overused, by the new age journalists and the Sunday-morning quarterbacks and recently by a former President, that it lost its true meaning, any value at all that might come attached to it all but stripped. But there was something so terribly pained in the eyes of the face in his scope, something way beyond and so far out there to Bolan, he found himself balking for a moment. Jenkins was smiling, stretched out, as if inviting Bolan to squeeze the trigger, apparent to him the man was struggling to come to terms with some torment.

Profound.

Whatever the man's demons, Bolan set him free, drilling a .308 round between the eyes. If there was someone waiting and willing to listen on the other side, Bolan wished him well. Confession of the soul and granting absolution for a man's wrongs were someone or something else's department.

He couldn't spare Jenkins another thought. Bolan still had the living and the angry to deal with.

The Executioner scanned the flaming earth and perimeter. He counted up six enemy shadows, scattering in all directions as they closed on the foothills. He made out Poe, sticking to the plan, it looked, as he bored for the swirling palls of black smoke to the north. The shadow man was lost to sight for several moments as he plunged into the smoke, then resurfaced near Bolan's latest body count. Poe lingered over the corpses, kills confirmed, then moved out.

The Executioner was wondering where the military's favorite slugger was. He strained his ears at the next rumble in the sky. No way to accurately gauge the altitude, but the flying monster was way up there, a massive blot beneath the stars. It was rolling in, still a mile or so to the southwest, when the wing pylons started the show for what he reckoned would be the curtain call, at least on the aerial end of it.

Mop up was next.

Bolan figured it best to ride out the coming storm before venturing into the inferno, and hugged the ground.

THE SMOKING CRATER saved his life, but it was by pure accident and clumsiness that Decker found himself plunging into the pit. Two clips, something like nine or ten guys shot up during his flight, and now he was somewhere near the western end of town.

Or what was left of Madjik.

There was more rubble, more bodies and body parts strewed along his march. He couldn't imagine anything surviving what the flying death machines had unloaded. And there was still more to come, as he somehow pinpointed the familiar thunder of the B-52, the mother of all bombers bearing down, ready to break open the earth once again.

He was running, bounding up and over another jagged heap of rubble, when the B-52 jump-started the terrible pounding. Looking back, he spotted a few shadows crawling out from under their blanket of rock. The first few explosions erupted a block east. He figured he'd better find the closest cover, hold on for dear life. Another step forward found him falling into darkness. The fireworks washed an eerie light over his descent, Decker letting himself free fall, knowing any uncertainty was preferable to getting squashed by a 2,000-pound gravity bomb.

He slammed down the side of the crater, flopping over slabs of stone, ricocheting off something meaty and wet, a whole range of noxious smells sweeping into his nose. The thunder followed him all the way down, seemed to ratchet up a few more earsplitting decibels even as he hit bottom, looked up to find the sheet of smoke holding over top, a lid to his tomb.

And death was what Decker found all around him.

There was no way of telling how large, or how many families even, had seen their last moments together before the bombs landed them here in the mass impromptu grave. He gagged as the miasma with its short list of poisonous smells seemed to swell his brain and dump the rest of him on a carousel.

Then the sky opened above the pit, pelting him with long showers of stone, body parts and whatever else. It sounded like the end of the world beyond his hole.

THE CLEANUP, as expected, was messy, pure butcher's work. The first two armed shadows staggered out of the smoke, one of them minus an arm, cleaved off at the shoulder, pumping a scarlet stream when Bolan held back on the trigger of his assault rifle, dropped them, not missing a step, and kept on rolling.

Bolan had wrapped up his sniping chore a good thirty minutes ago, all Taliban rabbits accounted for, the way cleared for a long, hard run across the tableland into the fire. He was sticking as best he could to the marching path prescribed by Poe, scouring the smoke to his right—the north—when another armed amputee slithered into sight.

The face of agony searched out the big man in black, the assault rifle lifted in trembling hands. He was missing both legs from around midthigh, but incredibly enough his turban was in full wrap, immaculate and untouched. Different circumstances, and Bolan would have found the sight some hideous caricature. He emptied a short burst into the face.

Moving on.

By the time he had marched away from the nearest fury of one inferno's tentacles, skirting the crackling wrath of another firestorm, he was drenched in sweat. The M-16 leading the way, he kept scouring the wasteland of torn bodies, bypassing the jagged hills where stone dwellings had just stood, selecting a less bumpy course over fairly even ground.

"Belasko! Over here!"

He homed in on Poe's voice and cut to his right, the shadow man standing on the other side of a ring of fire. He had company. The new guy on the block was gagging, wiping bile off his mouth, shaking his head to clear out the cobwebs, his bell sorely rung, no doubt, by the falling wrath of the Stratofortress.

"This is Decker," Poe said, his man in-country giving Bolan a nod.

Poe kicked at a severed head, sent it rolling a few feet in Bolan's direction. "Say hello to Colonel Khandar. May he rest in pieces."

So, Bolan thought, that was that. Or was it?

"You get what you came here for?" the soldier asked Poe.

"Most of it. A few loose ends are still wandering about."

"The Saudi." Decker filled in after a brief bout of hacking. "Left town. Word is he's buried so deep in the Khyber Pass—"

"Nothing short of a nuke will get him." Poe chimed in.

"And the Iranian?"

Poe pointed toward the foothills. "I've already called it in. Seemed he did want to do business with the old man—nice shots again, by the way. Anyway, paranoia got the best of our boy at the last minute. The Taliban was standing in, feeling it out. Decker here helped get the bad feelings stirred up, tossed a couple of grenades to get the party on the ground started."

A neat package, all wrapped up, nice and tight, Bolan thought. He searched their smudged, sweaty faces, thinking there had to be more here, but gave it up, grunting instead, searching the smoking ruins for any meandering Taliban. Poe and Decker were pros at hiding the truth, he decided, had probably spent most of their adult lives covering up, stabbing backs, burying bodies, weaving yarns of half-truths, at best, to cover the stink of their own sordidness and corruption.

"So, this is it?" Bolan asked.

"Not really," Poe answered. "Let's get the hell outta here before the stink even gets to me. We still need to march up the hills and make sure the Iranian at least has been sent to Allah. Or what's left of him."

Bolan filled the M-16 with a fresh clip. "Lead the way."

THE ENCORE STRAFING of the mountain didn't quite match the Apocalyptic intensity that had laid waste to Madjik, but Bolan chalked it up to his nagging sense that some riddle would never get solved. When the bombs stopped raining and the B-52 thundered on from its cleanup position, the soldier trailed Poe and Decker up a path he figured was already scoped and known to the shadow men. Not more than a dozen yards climbing, and the bodies and torn limbs started littering the way. Enough firelight outlined the shadows above them, guys scrambling down the mountainside, shouting in Farsi.

They were on a collision course. Unaware in their panic, hope or sense of relief they'd been spared death from above, they were lined up for easy pickings. Bolan had the range marked off, the Iranians descending from a hanging cloud of smoke, and cut loose with his M-16. The Executioner got their attention right away as two out of ten shadows screamed and pitched out of sight down some narrow opening to their side. Poe took care of three more Iranians, the HK-69 spitting a round up the incline, the grenade dumped in the heart of the trio just behind them, the explosion hurling bodies in free fall down the mountain, limbs as limp as pasta slapping off a jagged ledge in meaty thuds. From where the Iranians stood there appeared no cover, not even a solitary boulder. Decker joined in with his subgun, matching Bolan's bloody erasure of two more hardmen. It was over before they even got off the first round from their AK-47s.

Poe's search to confirm the big kill took a good twenty minutes. Bolan followed them up the path nature had carved in the mountain.

They found the Iranian staring at the sky near the mouth of a cave. He was sawed in two, intestines curling out, glistening like a gaggle of yellow eels as they reflected the distant inferno. It occurred to Bolan that Poe had known exactly where the Iranian and his brothers-in-jihad had been hiding all along. He gave their initial fire point a search. The jeep was hidden beyond a rocky ledge a good two thousand yards below and to the south. Still...

"I honestly didn't know they were here, Belasko," Poe told him, "until they were marked on Firebird One's screens. Yeah, I know. A wandering Iranian up here maybe just watching the show could have made his way down and nailed us. What can I say? Somebody somewhere liked us tonight."

It sure wasn't the way Bolan did business, winging it, and he found himself suddenly wishing for little more than to see a familiar friendly face.

"He sure doesn't look like the most wanted terrorist next to the Bin-meister now, does he?" Poe said, grinning at the Iranian's remains. "Too bad about the Saudi. He got lucky. Maybe next time."

The smoke climbed all around Bolan, blotting out the stars. There was heat still emanating from the surface where the explosions had given this stretch of mountain some thorough eco-terrorizing.

Bolan skipped the litany of questions he had for Poe. It would be enough to get out of Afghanistan and on their way, presumably to that classified base in Saudi Arabia. If nothing else, he needed to contact Brognola, aware that his old friend would be worried sick.

"Let's go home, Belasko. We're not finished. There's some brass still on the loose, the ones who sponsored the old man. The one who put together this whole black Hellbox project. He's some two-war four-star hero from the Pentagon. His name is Conroy."

17

The road to this particular hell led to the Outer Banks of North Carolina. According to Poe, the Void—as he tagged the four-man sponsorshop behind the late Raven—were waiting in their beachfront retreat for an update on why the bottom fell out on the Afghan deal, all hands nervous, Bolan was informed, wondering where it went from there.

The final four had run for cover in hurricane country. And Bolan was going in for the hard charge, gale-force style, nothing fancy. Stealth was out of the question anyway, since it was the middle of the afternoon, the sky washed blue, the sun blazing on the white sandspit where the traitors were nesting in their split-level digs.

Between the hours spent on the ground at the classified Saudi base—phoning home via secured satlink to Brognola, the big Fed heaving a sigh of relief at the first sound of Bolan's voice—then the transatlantic flight where Poe mapped out the last leg of the journey, landing them at a small private airfield in Camden, where the three of them loaded up their gear and weapons and boarded an SUV, motoring down 158, then NC 12, which linked the barrier islands.

Forget about it, Bolan told himself. This sojourn had nearly circled the planet, with missing hours enough, the soldier shoved into limbo, nearly one full day he knew of lost to coma. And the time it took to get to this next strike point was another annoying stretch, with Bolan putting the key questions to Poe, getting spoon-fed what sounded like all the right answers, strictly need-to-know.

More shadow chess.

But when he'd first learned about General Conroy and the assembly of rats, Bolan determined he was going the distance, bent on wrapping up the next piece of business his way. If Poe was setting him up, he'd know soon enough, and there would be an answer. For the time being he accepted that he would probably never know the full truth about the Hellbox conspiracy. Maybe later, when the smoke cleared and Brognola and the Farm could run their own investigation, root out any other snakes in the hole. First he needed to take out four major problems and their batch of shooters.

"So, that's how you want to do it? Charge the trench?"

Bolan kept the M-16 on the seat within easy reach. "Only six shooters on-site?"

Poe grinned into the rearview mirror. "Between you, the Taliban and our flyboys their roster's been trimmed to a skeleton crew of second stringers."

Bolan listened as Poe dialed up the radio receiver fixed to the dashboard. He didn't bother asking how, when or why the shadow man had bugged the place, since Poe would probably give him the usual look meant to tell Bolan he had his ways and was motivated purely in the interest of national security. He saw the face and heard that three times already on the flight back to the States. The guy, Bolan had long decided, had proved some piece of work, a BS master who'd honed his craft.

"I don't like this."

"That's their boy from FEMA," Decker told Bolan from the passenger seat, the soldier grimly aware Poe's buddy had an HK MP-5 subgun in his lap.

"He's always been the whiner of the bunch," Poe said. "Amazes me how guys like that ever get to claim the crown, first-class tickets the whole ride. First sign of trouble, they're ready to crack under the strain, cut and run."

Which made the men inside the beach house all the more dangerous, Bolan knew. They had everything to lose, their lives included.

"Someone's onto us, I tell you. I thought you said the old man had all the bases covered. I mean, there's only so much smoke I can blow the nuclear energy people's way about the blast we set off, some of my people on the Hill sniffing my way already. And that was something else I told you I had a problem with. Now, if what we're hearing is true, we'll never see a dime of the Iranian's money. Meaning no new shop, no factory for the devices...."

"Enough."

"Conroy," Poe said.

The four-star wonder, who, Bolan had been told, worked out of a covert crucible at the Pentagon, had jerked all the right strings with the politicoes to get the Hellbox project situated, on his own terms, of course. A longtime pal of the late old man. War buddies.

"We already have another prospective buyer lined up," Bolan heard the general state. "Funds are being gathered now. The necessary product will get funneled through our usual channels."

"Some country in the Middle East," a new voice said, "with the right amount of money, with the proper size chip on its shoulder toward its neighbors."

"The general's version of his own Raven sidekick," Poe said. "A floater. Calls himself, get this, Riddler. Not even I could tell you who exactly he belongs to."

The general said, "Specifically a grudge against the Saudis, a seething jealousy about their vast petroleum wealth. We get them to act on our behalf, well, when the devices start dropping them like flies, our own troops stationed there even falling to the radioactive Grim Reaper—but that goes without saying—by then we'll have a new force of our own signed up. March in. We'll own the oil fields with our new friends. Who's going to stop us? They'll be too sick, wondering why all the sudden invisible death."

The general laughed, a rolling noise, the source immensely pleased with itself, a familiar sound of evil believing it could own the world and use all its creatures for personal gain and pleasure striking an angry chord in the Executioner.

"Let's do it," Bolan said.

"Okay, but save the general for me, Belasko," Poe said. "He has vital information. It's squirreled away on a disk he has hidden somewhere in the house. The whole chalupa—names, places, who's been helping them smuggle out the waste from Los Alamos."

"I'm not making any promises. If it aims to shoot, I shoot back, four stars or four angels watching over the guy."

Poe didn't like it, scowling, but turned over the ignition. He snapped off the monitor after the man from FEMA whined, "Where is Poe, anyway?"

IT WAS CLEAR, as soon as Bolan stepped out of the SUV, the three hardmen hadn't expected a third arrival, and the sight of the Executioner raising an assault rifle their way dropped them into a blind panic. They were going for their MP-5s, the trio grouped to the side of a motor pool consisting of two SUVs and a Lincoln, one of them tossing down his handheld radio, when the soldier stitched them left to right with a long barrage that signaled the end was on the way for the masters of deceit.

Three down, three more to go, assuming Poe had told the truth. Bolan left Poe and Decker to charge the front steps, glimpsed another gunner barreling onto the porch, dropping under a curtain of twin lead storms chattering from the Colt Commando and MP-5.

Bolan went for the back door, the beach side, believing the sound of battle would drive the foursome to flee in that direction. Boots grabbing at loose sand, the soldier made the back edge.

Just in time to see the rats scurrying from their nest, as he hoped.

A nice neat package, wrapped up and dropped in his lap.

Two gunners were leading the exodus on a raised porch. Four men in suit jackets froze at the sight of Bolan, one of them crying, "You!"

The Executioner had a 40 mm grenade down the M-203's chute. They were clustered, frozen in place, and Bolan figured why make it any harder on himself than he had to. Poe would just have to find his Pandora's box of intel vital to national security the old-fashioned way, meaning he'd have to rifle through the works and gut the place by hand.

The gunners nearly got their act together, bringing up their subguns, but Bolan, aiming for the edge of a wood-pillared awning above the pack, sent the Hell bomb flying. At least three of the big four were beating it back inside the house when the blast sheared away a chunk of the wall. A brief scream trailed one of the hard-men as he was launched over the railing. Bolan bounded up the stairs, sighted two more victims—a gunner and a guy whose white-sheened hundred-dollar haircut was partly dyed red—and kept charging.

Two suits were picking themselves up, hacking and floundering on rubbery legs beyond the pall of smoke. They went for a final desperate stand, swinging Berettas toward the big harnessed invader, when Bolan let them have it, point-blank, up the ribs and coring his rising burst of autofire through their skulls.

"Don't shoot! We can reason this out, whoever you are, Belasko!"

Bolan recognized Conroy's voice, stepped around the bodies, boots crunching debris. The general's hands were thrust above his head, the man with the plan clearly afraid but clinging to whatever hope, dignity and respect he felt owed him, Bolan guessed, to a man who had served his country and climbed the ranks of power to become lord and master over all the little people. Few things sickened Bolan more than a traitor.

"Don't kill him, Belasko!"

Poe and Decker rolled into the living room, weapons holding at some point between the general and Bolan.

"Why did you do it, Poe?" Conroy snarled. "Dammit, man, we could have owned the world. I never should have trusted any floating operative. Who do you really work for, Poe? NSA? CIA?"

"I work for Uncle Sam."

"How about you, Belasko? That was quite the show you put on in New Mexico. How much to get you on the team?"

"I'm not for sale."

"For some reason, I'm not surprised."

"Where's your exortion ace, Conroy?" Poe demanded.

"No way. You'll have to kill me first. That's my only ticket to ride."

No warning, and Poe tapped the trigger on his assault rifle, chopped Conroy off at the knees. The general went down hard, cursing and howling.

"You bastard! Now I'll never tell you."

Torture never had a place in Bolan's battle scheme. More often than not, inflicting pain on unarmed prisoners was a tool used by the perpetrator to cut loose with some sadistic streak. A power thing.

The way Bolan saw Conroy was bleeding, he didn't think the man would last but a few minutes at best. Bolan made a decision based on the fact he didn't like Poe, for one thing, wanted to push the envelope and see if the guy would let his weapon do the squawking. And number-two reason for the final judgment was Bolan detested any man who would sell out his own, whatever the reason. The Executioner put Conroy out of his misery, M-16 stammering, marching a 3-round burst to shred the white sports shirt side to side.

Danger flared in Poe's eyes the next moment. The M-16's clip nearly burned through, aware he'd never have time enough to load a fresh magazine if Poe and Decker erupted, the soldier drew the big Desert Eagle. The shadow men hesitated long enough, indecision about something in their eyes, and Bolan had a bead locked on to Poe's face with the hand cannon's muzzle.

"That was dumb, Belasko. He was worth more alive than getting sent to the great void beyond. You know how many secrets just went skipping out of here, Chief?"

"Conroy can discuss it all with his friends in hell. I'm walking. I'm taking one of their vehicles. If what you want is here, I'm sure a little sweat will pay off."

"It's a big house, Chief, a half dozen safes to be cracked that I know of, maybe another half dozen stash points they kept to themselves. I could be here for days if Conroy's buried it. Hell, for all I know, he dug a hole in the sand. Wait a second, I get it now. I see you— snatching victory from the jaws of defeat. If you couldn't have it, I couldn't, either."

"Believe what you want."

"Then why? I thought, after all we've been through, we were on the same side."

"The only side in this thing is my own."

"What?" Decker got some attitude. "You shot him to spite us? Got squeamish 'cause the guy was in a little pain?"

"Like some smoke you've blown in my face, leaving me to wonder, I'll keep the answer to myself."

"The general always leaves the keys in the Lincoln. Get the hell outta my face, Belasko," Poe growled.

He couldn't wait to clear out, best news yet to Bolan. The Executioner angled past the shadow men, the Desert Eagle covering his exit.

Poe couldn't resist a parting shot. "Hey, Belasko."

As he topped the steps to the hallway leading out of there, Bolan found the man grinning.

"We could meet again someday. You never know. Just saying, there's no hard feelings. Things happen. It worked out."

"Did it?"

"Yeah. I know there's a lot more going on. Your big questions weren't answered. All I can tell you, the old man was going for the money, but these guys here...you know, I've heard it told power can become bored with itself. It always needs more power, something bigger to feed its hunger. Never happy, but maybe that just says something about human nature. Bunch of kids playing grown-up, want our way or else. These guys, if they weren't stopped, had a plan, crazy as it sounds, to take the oil fields in Saudi, irradiate the whole damn country. The new sheikhs."

"I gathered as much. Dreams like that...well, I've sometimes heard things work out the way they should."

"Yeah, destiny and all that."

"Maybe. Or maybe it's something else."

"Maybe I'll be seeing you around. For a little more destiny, that is."

Bolan grunted, aware of the sardonic cut to his mouth. No snappy one-liner came to mind, and it was just as well.

The soldier walked. It would be a sweet change to breath some clean air, he decided, moving into the sunlight and a warm, salt-tanged breeze. The SUV first, to retrieve his war bag, then the Lincoln. A quick call to Brognola to make some flight arrangements, Virginia Beach with all its military bases about a ninety-minute or so drive north.

Going home.

Death might carry its own putrid stink, he thought, but Bolan knew there were other bad smells nearly as strong that senses sharpened by a lot of bad experiences could pick up with one whiff.

The Executioner picked up the pace for the SUV, free at last from shadow men and their dirty deeds, his nose clear of the rotting smell of corrupt souls.

Epilogue

"The President unloaded his own version of that B-52 over at the White House when he heard the details on my end, Striker. He passes on his 'profound relief' that you came out the other side on this thing. You can believe, for whatever it's worth at this late juncture, some real big heads are getting put on the chopping block as we speak and get ready to indulge a much-deserved juicy slab of prime rib."

Bolan sipped the cold beer Brognola had taken the liberty to order and have on hand when the soldier found his old friend waiting for him, two empty Heinekens on the table already down the hatch while the soldier had been en route on the drive from Reagan National. They had the balcony, the smoking side, to themselves with the exception of a young couple near the end where the two banquet rooms were stacked. Bolan had just beaten the clock to closing time, and the waiter hadn't looked terribly pleased to see him take the table until Brognola handed off a twenty spot to stick around and hold the attitude.

Bolan smiled at Brognola, felt every weary turn and bump in the road on this mission, but it had never felt better to sit still, not worry about his back and share a few moments with an old friend.

"I just happened to be the wrong apple falling from the wrong tree."

Brognola matched Bolan's smile. "Yeah, that's one way of putting it. The President didn't know about the covert bombing run on that camp. Word is a bunch of folks with lots of ribbons and medals got nervous about their own loose cannons running around doing their own thing. We still can't confirm the identities of this old man, or Poe, for that matter."

"And you probably never will."

"Another thing that chaps me. That taste of Armageddon you saw over there was the Pentagon's show, the way I heard it. You can believe some heads are going to roll for a long time in that direction. The smoke will still be hanging probably come next election. Careers all but down the toilet, guys running for cover all over this town, damage control like you couldn't believe to keep the Afghanistan misadventure from the press. The President didn't know a damn thing about these Hellboxes either, but there was no reason he should. He's cutting loose a special team of his own to investigate and monitor closely any future so-called black projects."

"Maybe he'll let us know what's really out there in Roswell. Maybe he'll even invite a little gray man to dinner some time. Maybe the others have the secrets to the universe and can offer him the keys to the kingdom, a sort of campaign contribution in the form of eternal wisdom and knowledge."

Brognola had to have thought Bolan was serious for a moment, then studied the wry glint in the soldier's eye. Bolan wrote off the spook talk to spending too much time with Poe, some form of contamination that only time and distance would erase.

"I hear you, Striker. For all the good it'll do, but the Man figures he has to do something, just in case some guy with a camera and nothing better to do than chase phantoms starts burning up center stage on those nightly talking head shows. At any rate, our people were unable to confirm much more than the crater that showed up in New Mexico through their usual channels, sat imagery, mainframe theft. Ten kilotons went off underground. I still don't understand why they did it, blowing up their own factory, and even if this Conroy could ring the whole Saudi border with Hellboxes...our people can't find the first spec on the thing."

"I never saw it, either. But it was apparently worth the opposition's dying over."

"I guess we'll never know the answers to our bigger questions."

"It happens like that."

"I hate mysteries."

They shared a comfortable silence as only two men who were friends and who had known each other as long as they had could. The waiter grew antsy, came and took their order. Two king cuts of prime rib, medium rare, sounded good to Bolan, suddenly aware he hadn't eaten in days. They were breaking down the salad bar when Brognola suggested they'd better go there and load up.

Bolan didn't move right away, again looking Brognola dead in the eye, thinking it felt good to smile and feel it from the heart. "It's nice to sit here and not worry about keeping my back to the wall or wonder how many lies and half-truths I'm supposed to swallow."

"That's what friends are for. You know, I haven't said it yet, but it's damn good to see you, Striker. All of us were getting real concerned when it looked like you vanished into thin air."

"Appreciate the sentiments, Hal, all around, thanks." Bolan killed his beer. "I was becoming a little concerned myself."

"Let's eat. Enjoy the moment."

They stood and made their way downstairs, Bolan thinking the simple things in life were often the sweetest. In his world, he never knew if there'd be another moment to enjoy. A heartbeat too slow here, a fraction of an inch there, and he would, indeed, vanish off the face of the earth.

But not tonight. Tomorrow would arrive soon enough, and the soldier would march back out there to slay the next dragon or get burned in the process. Whatever waited, it was on hold for now as he trailed his old friend to the salad bar. Sometimes, he decided, living in a moment like this was good enough, or at the least as good as it would get.

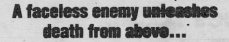

James Axler

OUTLANDERS®

PRODIGAL CHALICE

The warriors, who dare to expose the deadly truth of mankind's destiny, discover a new gateway in Central America—one that could lead them deeper into the conspiracy that has doomed Earth. Here they encounter a most unusual baron struggling to control the vast oil resources of the region. Uncertain if this charismatic leader is friend or foe, Kane is lured into a search for an ancient relic of mythic proportions that may promise a better future…or plunge humanity back into the dark ages.

In the Outlands,
the shocking truth is humanity's last hope.